AND JESUS
CAME BACK

JOHN BRUNI

www.roosterrepublicpress.com

AND JESUS CAME BACK

A NOVEL BY
JOHN BRUNI

"You gotta be one of the good guys, son: 'cause there's way too many of the bad."

-Garth Ennis, *Preacher* #9

CHAPTER 1: THE RETURN

"Gosh darn it!"

Old Joe MacDonald sucked in a breath and held his throbbing thumb. He didn't want to look at it, but he had to see how bad it was. Squinting and looking—against his better judgment—he saw the giant splinter sticking out from under his thumbnail. Blood welled up under the cuticle in a diaphanous red cloud.

Holy heck, it looked crazy. Gritting his teeth, he grabbed the end of the splinter and pulled it out as quickly as he could, flinging it aside. Blood oozed out, and he stuck his thumb in his mouth, sucking on it.

Served him right. He should have been wearing gloves. He'd just forgotten them back at the house. He didn't want to walk the mile just to get them. His back, humped by his age and vocation, probably couldn't take it.

It could have been worse, he supposed. He only had two fingers on that hand in addition to the thumb. The others had been lost in an accident when his hand had gotten caught in a mower. One of the survivors had also been chopped off, but the doctor managed to reattach that one. It hurt him on rainy days, even though it had happened twenty years ago.

He took his thumb out of his mouth and examined it. Gave it a squeeze. Even though the nail still looked beet red, blood no longer came out of the wound. He'd have Ursula look at it when he finished up with this darned post.

He didn't know how the heck those kids had managed to knock it out of place. They weren't that big, and they couldn't possibly have the strength it took to do something like this. Sure, the fence had gotten rickety over the years, but it shouldn't have been weak enough to topple under the weight of a couple of ten-year-old boys.

Heck with it. He wrapped his hands around the wood—this time being mindful of splinters—and rocked it back and forth, stretching it against the barbed wire that still connected it to the rest of his fence. Sweat beaded on his forehead and ran coldly down his back. He could feel it collecting in the neckline of his shirt and between his legs. He couldn't wait for a shower.

Soon, flies and bees were replaced by mosquitoes and lightning bugs, but he didn't notice, not even as the world darkened and night eased across the sky. As he struggled with the fence post, he thought about his station in life. There weren't too many independent farmers like him left in the world. Even though he knew pride was a sin, he couldn't help but feel proud of himself. Who wanted to knuckle under the godless government? Sure, the money from government subsidies would be good, but there were more important things in the world than money.

He had his soul, and that made him feel good about himself. About his work. About his family.

Times were getting tougher, though. This work never got easier, especially as he clocked more years on his body. He felt like an old man at fifty-nine. His leathery dark skin showed deep seams caused by too much time out in the elements. Hard work made his body even harder, but it did nothing for his creaking joints. At least he could say he still had most of his teeth, although a few of the ones up front were missing and very noticeable.

He should have started his family earlier. How did he expect to keep up with kids at this age? He didn't know how Ursula managed to stay so strong. At least the kids were coming of age, and they'd be good for field work soon. They had to be ready, or they might lose the farm. He didn't think he could handle that, not after a lifetime of toil. He refused to be the one who lost the family property. This land had been theirs as far back as the War of 1812. If they lost it because of him—

Well, he didn't want to think about that. It might lead to something sinful.

Finally, he leaned on the post, freshly planted, and it didn't move in the slightest. Solid work. He brushed his diminished hand across his forehead and over his thick grizzled beard. Only then did he notice how dark the sky had gotten. The galaxy swirled majestically above him, the last of the day fading to the west, the color of a dying ember. It illuminated the forest in the distance, the trees standing out by their stark blackness against the last of the sun. He reached into the pocket of his overalls for his grandfather's watch and opened the cover. Shocked at how much time had slipped by him, he realized how hungry he was. Ursula was probably wondering what had happened to him.

He wiped his wet hands on his overalls and bent over to pick up his tools. His back wanted to lock up when he tried to straighten, but he waited for it to get used to the idea of moving. Slowly he pulled himself up to as much of his full height as he could, and he started walking back to the house.

Yes, he thought, feeling the ache of work settling in his bones, times were tough. Faith was hard to maintain. Hope swirled at the bottom of the drain. But he still had life.

He looked up, closing his eyes, and said a quick prayer to the Lord, thanking Him for another day and hoping for yet another. "Amen," he whispered.

Just then, he opened his eyes and saw an odd light in the sky. It seemed to be getting bigger, and he wondered if it might be a plane. But no, this thing moved too erratically to be a plane. He squinted, trying to get a better look at it. Could it be a shooting star?

It whistled overhead, and Joe dropped down to his knees, the hairs on his neck sticking up as if he'd almost been struck by lightning. Then he heard an explosion, and the ground shook hard enough to knock him over. Breathing heavily, he pushed himself up, struggling to his feet. He could smell sulfur in the distance, and he knew—just *knew*—that whatever it was, it had come down on his land.

Smoke rose against the glow on the horizon, and it looked like it might be a half-mile away. He could make that. It would be a bit hard on his knees, but he thought he should check it out.

Ordinarily he would have put it off until the next day, when he could bring his kids with. But the smell and the smoke said otherwise. He didn't want this thing to burn his crops. That would be just perfect, wouldn't it? If he lost so much as a corn stalk . . .

As he made his way, limping slightly, he didn't really wonder what might have come crashing down on his land. He'd never harbored curiosity in his heart. All he needed to know about the world, he found in his Bible, which he read from every night before he went to sleep. A few years ago he found out that the public school had tried to teach his kids that humans were descended from monkeys. Hogwash. He pulled them from classes immediately and home-schooled them. No child of his would ever be poisoned with such garbage.

In this moment he only knew that this punishment from the stars might ruin his crops, and he couldn't have that. Practicality trumped curiosity every time.

He pushed through the corn stalks, and the burning smell grew stronger. He could see flickering light ahead, and he knew he'd lost some of the crop. Even from this distance he could hear corn kernels popping.

"Gosh darn it," he muttered.

And then he came to where the corn stalks had been scorched and torn away. Whatever had crashed had carved a crater out of the ground about eight feet deep and fifteen wide. Popcorn burned in the fire that blazed from the depths of this hole. He peered down into the smoke and fire, holding a hand over his mouth and nose. He saw . . . no. That couldn't be possible.

It looked like there might be a man in there.

Joe hacked out a few coughs, and he spat. Even in the dark he could see his saliva had been darkened. "There someone in there?" he called out.

"Yeah. Help me up." A pale sooty hand reached out of the fire, but it didn't look like the skin was burned. Something had put a hole through his wrist, though.

Joe would have to bring him back to the house, where he had a first aid kit. He reached through the smoke and grabbed the hand, pulling up with all his might. His back buckled a little—and his joints burned—but he still had enough strength in his hard body to pull this stranger from the hole.

The man came up easily, and much to Joe's surprise he also came up naked. The skinny stranger stood in the middle of the cornfield, shaking his wild-maned head as if to clear his mind of any kinks. A beard covered a great deal of his bony chest, but not so much that it hid a savage gash in his side. Yet no blood came from the wound. Thinking back Joe didn't think the hole in the guy's wrist bled, either.

And the stranger's . . . well, Joe turned away from that. The stranger certainly packed a more impressive tool than Joe did, and Joe considered himself a large man.

"Thanks, friend," the stranger said. "Sorry I tore up your field a bit, but I've come a long way, and there's just not a gentler way of arriving. I'm Jesus. Jesus Christ. Nice to meet you." He held out his hand as if to shake.

Joe stared at the offered hand, looking from it to Jesus' eyes. Suddenly a smile cracked Joe's seamed face practically in two, and he let out a hardy guffaw.

Puzzled, Jesus lifted an eyebrow, scratching at the back of his head. "Did I say something funny?"

Joe's laughter died down, and he pointed at the newcomer. "I'm no priest, kid, but I'm pretty sure the son of God wouldn't fall from the sky like some half-baked Superman, and he certainly wouldn't land on my farm in his birthday suit."

Jesus shrugged. "You've got a point, I

guess. It's just that it's a long fall from Heaven, and we don't wear clothes up there. Don't need 'em."

Joe snapped his fingers as he remembered something he'd been taught as a kid at Sunday school. "Shouldn't you be talking old-timey?"

"How do you mean?"

"I'm pretty sure no one spoke English back in the Biblical times."

Jesus slapped his forehead. "Ah! I get it. You've got it all wrong, Joe. Right now I'm speaking all languages. I think I'm speaking Hebrew, and I probably am, but you're going to hear me in whatever your native tongue is."

Joe missed most of that answer. His breath caught in his throat when he heard this stranger refer to him by name. He could even feel his own skin growing cooler as he paled. "How did you know my name?"

"I know everything about you, Joseph John MacDonald."

It couldn't be. Joe's mouth worked to form those words, but nothing came out. Instead he said, "You're a naked guy lost in my cornfield."

Jesus sighed, shaking his head. "Dad and I talk about this all the time. It's a shame that you guys rely so much on evidence rather than faith. Still, I guess that's what I'm here for this time. No one is ever going to need faith again, Joe. I'm here to give you all the answers you've ever wanted or needed."

A part of Joe wanted to believe this

stranger, but a side of himself that he liked to call "common sense" told him that this was impossible. Of course he believed in Jesus Christ. He just couldn't believe in *this* Jesus Christ.

"I know you're confused," Jesus said. "I know you doubt me. I'm here to remove all doubt from everyone's mind. I'm here to deliver the truth. You've lived a hard life, Joe. I'm here to help make it easier."

Slowly Jesus reached across the space between them, and Joe thought he could see a slight glow in this man's dark eyes. He thought it might be the reflection of the fire, but something about that explanation didn't feel right.

Jesus' hands touched each side of Joe's head. Joe had never been touched like this by another man, and it made him feel nervous. Maybe the stranger was a sodomite. The thought scared him enough to start him moving back, but Jesus held strong.

"Here's all the proof you need," he whispered.

Light flashed between Jesus' fingers and from his eyes and mouth. His hair stood out, as if he'd stuck his finger in a light socket. Joe straightened out, shocked. He felt no pain, but he felt . . . *something*. Something changed inside of him, but he couldn't understand what.

The light intensified, and it hurt to look at it. Joe squeezed his eyes shut, but it didn't help much. So much brightness made it past his eyelids that he wondered if he was dreaming.

His eyes rolled back, and Jesus released him. Joe fell to the ground, smoke drifting off his ears. "What . . . did you do . . . to me?"

"Rise, Joseph John MacDonald. See for yourself."

Joe didn't think he'd be able to stand up, but much to his surprise he felt a spring in his bones. His joints didn't creak as he neatly jumped to his feet. How could this be possible?

And then he realized he stood a head and shoulders above Jesus. Before, he'd been on eye level with the stranger. Joe stretched back and realized his hump was gone, as if it had never been there. Shocked, he looked to his hands. The wound from the splinter had healed completely, and he now had all of his fingers.

He touched his mouth, and his missing teeth had been restored. For the first time in years he was a complete man.

This *had* to be a dream.

"It's no dream," Jesus said. "This is all real."

Joe felt his eyes burn, and he suddenly realized that he'd been crying for at least a minute. Tears cut down his cheeks—no longer craggy but smooth, almost like new flesh—and he felt his chest hitch. Words couldn't pass through his clogged throat in a million years.

He gave in and fell to his knees before Jesus, sobbing. "Forgive me, Lord. I didn't mean to doubt."

Jesus pulled Joe to his feet, annoyed. "No more of that. The time for supplication is over. I'm here to change all of that."

Joe couldn't bring himself to look into the eyes of his savior, not after he'd failed the Lord so spectacularly. Hadn't St. Peter denied Christ three times? Joe didn't think he'd gone that far, and he silently thanked . . . well, he thanked the man in front of him.

"Why me?" Joe asked.

"Why you what?" Jesus asked.

"Why did you choose me out of all the people in the world? You could have revealed yourself to the President of the United States. Or the Pope. You could have come to earth anywhere. You chose my farm."

Jesus grimaced, as if he'd just caught whiff of road kill on a summer day. For a second he opened his mouth, as if to say something, but he closed it again as if he didn't know what to say. Then: "I hate to disappoint you, but not everything is planned. It was just the luck of the draw. No plan on that one."

"It couldn't be random. You're the son of God. You're proof of order in the world, not chaos."

"Well, I'd love to argue the point, but it's kind of chilly out. I don't suppose you have pants I could use, do you? And uh, I don't mean to impose, but it's been a couple thousand years since the last time I was here. I'm probably waaaaaaaay behind on my rent. Think I could stay with you? At least for tonight?"

Joe didn't hesitate. He unbuckled the

straps of his overalls and dropped them. He stepped free from the garment and scooped it up, handing it to Jesus.

"You can stay with me forever, if you want," Joe said. "As long as I have a roof over my head, so do you, my Lord."

"Enough with that Lord stuff. Call me Jesus." He took the overalls and put them on. They hung off him, considering how skinny he was compared to Joe's bulk.

Joe stood before him, wearing nothing but a ratty, checkered shirt and his tighty-whities. "Come home with me, Jesus. I want to introduce you to my family."

Jesus grinned. "Joe, my friend, you seem to forget. I already know them."

He waved a hand, and the burning corn stalks—Joe had forgotten about them—hissed and died, leaving nothing but smoke and a burned odor.

The two of them walked side by side through the cornfield. Joe didn't have to lead his new companion. It was as if Jesus already knew the way. For a while, they continued in silence, but as they started down the path that led to the house, Joe found himself uncomfortable at the lack of conversation. He'd loved Jesus since his parents taught him about his savior as a child. Now that he stood in the presence of his Lord, why couldn't he think of something to say?

He cast his mind back to what they'd said to each other so far, and he finally found something to latch onto. "You said something back there, Jesus. I don't mean to pester you any, but do you think you could explain it?"

"I'll do my best."

"You said no one is ever going to need faith again. What did you mean by it?"

"Last time, I was here to die for your sins. This time, I'm here to reveal the truth. You don't need faith to believe in truth. Truth is truth. To all the atheists and agnostics, to everyone who ever wanted proof of God, here I am. I'm going to heal this world, I'm going to mend it, to make it whole once again, even if I have to lay hands on each and every single one of you."

Joe stared, dumbfounded. Could it be that he'd lived long enough to see paradise on earth? How could he have been so lucky? "That's . . . that's beautiful, Jesus. Thank you."

Jesus slapped him on the shoulder. "It's what I'm here for, buddy."

A few minutes later they both stood outside Joe's farmhouse. The lights blazed from within, and they could hear the TV blaring. The kids liked it too darned loud. He'd have to talk to them about that.

But later.

"Wait right here," Joe said. "I just want to explain what's going on before I bring you in. Okay?"

"Take your time," Jesus said. "I'm not going anywhere."

Joe thumped up the porch steps, still surprised that his joints didn't try to fold in on themselves, and walked across the creaking floorboards to the front door. He passed through, and his eyes moved over the quaint living room. They'd never had much money, so they couldn't afford gimcracks and geegaws like plasma screen TV's. The one they had was an old fashioned Zenith from the 'Sixties, one that stood on four legs and had no buttons, just two knobs to the right of the screen. The twins—Ethan and Allen— watched an old rerun of a popular western, but they seemed more interested in the toys strewn about them on the carpet.

In the corner a stout, middle-aged woman sat in a rocking chair, knitting. Times had been rough for her, too. Arthritis had gnarled her hands, so today must have been a good day; her fingers moved almost nimbly. The gray hair at her temples spread, and her body, much like his own, had toughened with age but not in a good way. He remembered when he used to touch her in their youth, how soft her skin had been. Now when he caressed her, it felt like he was touching leather.

"Kind of late, isn't it, Joe?" Ursula asked.

"Something happened tonight. Something big."

Ursula looked up and nearly dropped her knitting. "Joe! Where are your overalls?!"

He turned to his sons. "Gather around, kids."

Ursula squinted up at his face now. "Is there something different about you? It's hard to see, the light's so dim in here, but—"

"I'll explain in a moment."

Ethan and Allen approached. Neither of them looked eager to be taken away from the

TV and their toys. But then, just before Allen had the chance to laugh at Joe's underwear, Ethan looked up at his father and gasped. "Daddy! Your hair!"

Ursula's eyes widened. "Did you get hair dye?"

Joe touched his hair. It had always been thick, even in his old age. Now he turned to a mirror on the wall. He kept it just by the door so he could give himself a once-over before facing the world. Instead of the salt-and-pepper he usually saw, he'd gone completely black, just like when he was a kid.

More: for the past twenty years, his face had been deeply lined and suntanned. Now it looked almost new, like he'd gotten a face lift. He still had color to his skin, but it no longer looked like an old ragged wallet.

"It makes you look so much younger," Ursula said.

Joe turned back to his wife. "It's not hair dye. It's so much better than that. Come outside with me." He offered her his hand.

She put her knitting aside, and with a withered, trembling hand she let him help her up. But something felt off. They hadn't done a lot of hand-holding lately, but they still did it on occasion, and she knew right away that his grip didn't feel right. She looked down to the knot their fingers made and saw it right away. She couldn't believe her own eyes. Shocked, she looked into her husband's face. "What's going on?"

"A miracle," Joe said. "Our lives have just changed forever. It's happening. It's finally happening."

Almost scared, she blinked as if to clear her eyes. "*What's* happening?"

Joe led her outside, onto the porch, and their kids followed. There he gestured to their guest. "He's returned. Just like they always said he would."

Ursula stared at Jesus, uncomprehending.

"It's him. Jesus Christ. He's back, and he healed me. He gave me my fingers back." He pulled his hand away from hers and wiggled flesh that hadn't been there a mere hour ago.

She touched her mouth, unable to breathe. "Jesus?"

Jesus grinned. "What's up, Mrs. MacDonald?"

Her knees buckled, and Joe caught her before she could collapse. She panted as he helped her straighten out. "Is this really happening, Joe? *Really*?"

The twins stepped around their parents and walked to Jesus, looking up at him, eyes wide. Ethan said, "Is it true?"

"Are you really him?" Allen asked.

"Sure am," Jesus said.

Ethan mouthed one word: "Wow." He looked away, as if digesting this information.

Allen didn't waver. "Prove it."

Joe glanced up at his sons. "Quit being a nuisance, boys."

Jesus waved a dismissive hand. "It's all right. Everyone's skeptical. That's what I'm here to end, remember?"

He disengaged from the twins and walked up to their parents. He held out a hand, smiling. "Let me touch you, Mrs. MacDonald."

Unable to speak, she just nodded.

Gently, Jesus placed his hands on either side of her head. Then, just as he had before with Joe, his eyes and mouth started glowing. Knowing what would happen next, Joe looked away. The air sizzled as if a lightning bolt had struck nearby, and Joe felt an electric shock run through him, just from touching Ursula.

He looked back, and the first thing he noticed was her hair. Just like his, it had gone a dark gray, and now it stood out as pure black. Wrinkles no longer cut so deeply into her face, and her flesh felt new under his touch.

Just like it had when they were younger.

"Flex your hands," Jesus said.

Ursula looked down at them and saw they no longer looked skinny and crooked. Strong and vibrant, she did what he asked and marveled when she didn't even feel a twinge of pain.

No more arthritis.

Jesus Christ had just cured her of arthritis.

Gaping, she looked up at her savior. He smiled back.

Allen stared, unbelieving. For almost as long as he could remember, his mother couldn't move her hands without wincing. Now she did so freely, a smile slowly spreading on her face. Something twinkled in her eyes. Allen didn't know what it was, but had he been older he would have recognized it right away: youth.

Ethan gave his brother a playful slap on the back of the head. "You had to doubt him."

Allen glared at him, but he didn't say anything.

"He's going to stay the night with us," Joe told his wife.

She looked at him as if he were crazy. "The son of the Lord? In *our* home?" She then broke away from him and rushed into the house. Almost right away he heard her turn on the vacuum. He started laughing.

"Dad, he can have my bed," Ethan said.

"No!" Allen said. "Let him have mine!"

"That's enough, boys. He's staying in mine. Go on to bed, all right?"

"But—" Ethan said.

"No buts. Go on."

Scowling, the twins stalked back into the house. Ethan, however, paused at the front door and turned back, looking at Jesus as if he couldn't believe it.

"Good night, Ethan," Jesus said.

Ethan's cheeks flared up bright red, and he scurried inside.

As soon as they were alone, Jesus turned to the renewed farmer. "I can't take your bed, Joe. Let me sleep in the stable."

"I won't hear of it."

"But—"

"No buts from you, either. What would I tell St. Peter if I let the son of God sleep in the barn?"

Jesus nodded. "Well, I appreciate it. It'll be nice to sleep in a bed. I never got to do that the last time I was here."

Joe clapped him on the back. "Rest up, Jesus. Tomorrow's going to be a big day for the both of us. I'm going to bring you to my church and introduce you to Reverend Potts. Something tells me he's been waiting a long time to meet you."

Jesus yawned, stretching. "That sounds great. I'm pretty beat. Travel always wipes me out. Show me the way to bed."

CHAPTER 2:
THE HEALING

T HUD! THUD! THUD!

"Hey Jesus! Wake up! It's chow time!"

Jesus opened his eyes and cast his gaze around the room. The MacDonalds' bed felt hard and lumpy, but it was one of the softest things he'd ever slept on. He felt completely refreshed as he swung out of bed, stood and walked naked to the door. He opened it and poked his head out.

Joe stood there and handed him a towel. "Bathroom's down that way, if you need to shower. Ursula will lay out some clothes for you when you're done."

Jesus wrapped the towel around himself. "Thanks, Joe."

"See you down in the kitchen for breakfast. Ursula cooks the best omelets."

Joe watched Jesus walk to the bathroom, and then he clomped down the stairs to the kitchen. Ursula fretted over the oven, practically in a panic. She dropped the wooden spoon she used to stir up a fresh batch of scrambled eggs. "Gosh darn it!" she said.

Joe stooped down and picked it up for her. "Relax, honey."

"What if he doesn't like my cooking?"

"Impossible." He kissed her. At first, he'd meant it to be a quick peck, but then he felt something soar in his heart. He kissed her deeply and swept her down in a romantic gesture. Laughing, she kissed him back.

"Joe! What's gotten into you?"

"Don't you feel it, too?" he asked.

"What?"

"Youth. We're young again. This was what it was like, remember?"

They heard the kids coming out of their room, so Joe straightened them both up and brushed off the front of her apron. He winked and turned to the table, sitting down.

Ethan and Allen rushed into the kitchen. "Where is he, Dad?" Ethan asked.

"Is he still here?" Allen asked.

"He's taking a shower," Joe said. "He'll be down soon. Then we'll all get dressed up and we'll head off to church. Speaking of clothes, Ursula, would you please—"

"I remember," she said. "I just don't know what to give him. It's not like we have holy robes or anything."

"I think a shirt and trousers would suffice," Joe said. "Mine might be a bit big on him, but I'm sure there's something he could wear."

Ursula finished with the eggs and distributed them to their respective plates, including one for Jesus at the head of the table where Joe usually sat. Then she wiped her hands off and went to their bedroom to fetch some clothes.

Joe fixed up some toast, and they ate silently. The boys kept watching the door, eager to see their Lord and savior again. Joe thought about what he'd tell the reverend when they saw him later. Maybe he should ask Mrs. Bradley to come along. She got around in a wheelchair with her daughter's help. It would probably be good to have her around so Jesus could prove himself to the reverend.

Ursula came back and went to work on an omelet. Just then Jesus showed up, his hair tied back in a wet ponytail. His beard still sparkled with beads of water. He wore an old button-down white shirt and a pair of pants Joe hadn't been able to fit into in ten years.

"How do I look?" Jesus asked.

"Very good," Joe said. "It must be weird. I know you're more used to robes."

"It's fine. Maybe a bit constrictive but not bad. I think I'm going to skip the robes this time around. It's a new world, and if I wore them it might be a bit, I don't know, over the top."

Joe nodded to the vacant seat. "Omelet's on the way."

"Thank you." Jesus sat and went to work on the eggs. Immediately he moaned. "This is great, Mrs. MacDonald. Absolutely divine."

"Please," she said, "call me Ursula."

"Ursula, then."

She brought the omelet to Jesus, who set in

right away. All eyes in the room turned to him, watching him eat. Everyone else forgot their own food for the moment.

Jesus peered up from his meal. "What?"

"It's a bit surreal," Joe said. "The son of God is eating breakfast with us."

"Don't think of me that way," Jesus said. "I'm just a guy like everyone else. For the most part, at least."

Joe opened his mouth, ready to disagree, but then he realized that Jesus had a point. They were all just staring at him eating, which was incredibly rude. He closed his mouth.

Later, he called Rev. Potts and the Bradley house to set everything up. After the table had been cleared, and everyone got dressed and ready, they piled into the family car—a rickety old Plymouth—and headed down to church.

They all met in the rectory. Mrs. Bradley beat them to it since she lived in town. She sat in her wheelchair, a hunched over, frail form. Her eyes looked beady and myopic behind her giant glasses. Carol Bradley stood behind her mother, leaning on the wheelchair's handles. Her stout frame showed very little fat, and her strong arms nearly bristled, a testament to the decades she'd been taking care of her mother.

Reverend Austin Potts sat behind his desk, corpulent and balding. A pair of spectacles hung off the end of his fat nose, but he rarely looked through them. When the MacDonalds arrived, he did not stand up to greet them. He welcomed them warmly, but he didn't put a lot of effort into it.

Joe reached across the desk and shook Potts's hand. "I'm glad you agreed to see us, Reverend. Something very important happened to me last night, something wonderful, and I have to share it with the world. You were the first person I thought of. After Ursula, of course."

"That's fine, son," Potts said, "but I still don't get why you wanted Mrs. Bradley and her daughter here."

"You'll see in a moment, but first I want to introduce my new friend." He turned and went to the door. He opened it and leaned out. "Come on in."

Jesus walked across the threshold, his hair now undone from the ponytail and framing his face like a lion's mane. The both of them approached the reverend's desk, and Jesus reached across, offering his hand.

Potts noticed the hole in Jesus' wrist, and he grimaced. Instantly he knew what this was.

"I know this is going to sound strange, but this is Jesus," Joe said.

Potts still didn't reach for Jesus' hand. He stared, his face turning red.

Jesus didn't pull back. "Nice to meet you, Austin. I've heard some nice things about you."

Finally Potts found his voice. "Is this some kind of joke?"

Nervous, Joe looked over his shoulder and saw his wife back there, a hand resting on each of their sons' shoulders. Both kids stared at the scene unfolding before them. To the side Carol looked confused. Her mother Agnes seemed not to notice anything.

He looked back to the reverend. "I swear to you he fell out of the sky on my property last night. He told me he was here to reveal to the world all the mysteries of our existence."

"No more faith needed," Jesus said. "You'll all have facts."

Potts snarled. "This isn't a joke. This is . . . blasphemy. I did not expect this from someone as devout as you, Joe."

"I have proof!" Joe held up his hands and waggled his fingers. "Notice anything new?"

Potts looked at Joe's hands, and a chill ran through his guts. Now he looked up to Joe's face, shocked to see how much younger his parishioner appeared. At first he'd thought it was just hair dye, but the fingers? Those couldn't be explained. Potts vividly remembered visiting Joe in the hospital after they'd been cut off in the accident.

Could plastic surgery explain this? He didn't think so, but the alternative didn't seem possible.

"I can see the disbelief on your face," Joe said. "That's why I asked for Mrs. Bradley to be here."

Potts's face jiggled like gelatin, and he practically spit. "That's outrageous! I refuse to have you turn my rectory into a faith healing demonstration!"

"Mrs. Bradley has been crippled with MS for the past, what? Twenty years? How long

32

has it been since she could control her own body? Don't you think she should be given the chance?"

"Have faith for one last time," Jesus said. "Then you won't ever have to again."

Potts looked at Carol. "What do you think?"

Carol's mouth worked for a moment as she tried to find the right words. A low whine came from the back of her throat as she glanced between Potts and Joe and Jesus. She couldn't believe any of this. It flew in the face of reason. But if there was anything that could help—*anything at all*—she couldn't turn away from it. She could barely remember a time in her life that she hadn't had to take care of her mother. She didn't have many friends, and she couldn't date. Who would want to saddle themselves with this situation?

She thought about the freedom she'd have and how nice it would be for her mom to be able to bathe herself and clean up after her own excretions.

"Please, Reverend," she said. "Let them try."

The sides of Potts's jaw pulsed, and it looked like he wanted to say more, to perhaps even verbally chastise a member of his flock for willingly buying into this garbage. Then, he sighed. His body was still wound tightly like a spool of thread, but he knew he had to let this happen.

"Very well," he said. "I trust everyone in this room will have the decency to not mention this incident to anyone when this display fails to bear fruit."

Jesus beamed. "Thanks, Austin."

Potts glared at him, but he didn't say anything.

Jesus crossed the room and stooped down next to Agnes so he could look her in the eyes. "Take it easy, Agnes. I'm here to help. Just take a breath and relax, okay?"

Her eyes flicked over to him, regarding him through her thick glasses. "You look familiar. Do I know you, young man?"

"Everyone knows me," Jesus said. He straightened up and extended both hands toward her head.

Joe looked away, and this time he noticed his family did, too, even Ethan and Allen, who had only witnessed it. The light didn't necessarily hurt, but it was so powerful it made one uncomfortable. They could see the room brighten, and then came the all-too-familiar sizzle. Potts cried out suddenly, and Carol gasped loudly.

When the room dimmed back to its ordinary state, Joe looked back to see Carol and Potts shielding their eyes. Jesus seemed deflated and out of breath as his hands dropped back.

Agnes, on the other hand, couldn't have looked better. Her white hair had been instantly restored to a youthful blonde, and the liver spots on her hands were gone. For the first time in his memory, Joe saw surprise on Agnes's face.

"You see?" Jesus asked. "Everything's okay now."

Agnes moved her hands—something that she hadn't done in a year—and gripped the arms of the wheelchair. Gingerly she pulled herself up, as if she expected pain to wrack her body at any moment. It did not, and she took three strong and even steps away from the contraption she'd been stuck in for two decades.

Carol covered her unhinged mouth, eyes wide.

Agnes reached up to the glasses on her face and cast them aside. "I can even see everything perfectly, like I have 20/20 vision. I've worn glasses since third grade."

Potts stared in awe, doubt completely erased from his face. He let his spectacles drop to his chest, held there by a loop around his neck.

Joe smiled at him. "Told you so."

"I can't . . ." Potts croaked and cleared his throat. "I . . . did this really just happen?"

"I've still got plenty of energy," Jesus said. "If you have any more sick people in need of healing, line 'em up. I'll take care of them all."

Potts stood so quickly his chair cracked against the wall behind him. He rushed around the desk and dropped to his knees in front of Jesus, pressing his forehead against the savior's feet. "Please, Lord. Forgive me. How was I to know?"

Jesus hooked a hand under Potts's arm and pulled him to his feet. "That's enough of that. And call me Jesus, willya? And it's okay. I get how hard this is for everyone. It's going to get very easy, very soon."

Sweat beaded on Potts's forehead and ran down one of his temples to his collar. "Jesus, I'm glad you're here. We do have a lot of sick people in our church, and I would appreciate it if you would go to work immediately."

Jesus clapped him on the shoulder. "That's what I'm here for. Call 'em down and we'll get this thing done."

"We'll start phoning everyone," Joe said. "Come on, Ursula. Kids."

"We'll help," Agnes said. She turned to Jesus. "Thank you. From the bottom of my heart, I owe you everything."

"Don't mention it," Jesus said.

He waited while the others filed out to find the community directory and some phones. As soon as he was alone with Potts, he turned to face the reverend. "There's just one more thing."

"Anything, Jesus," Potts said.

"I know what you've been fantasizing about," Jesus said.

Potts felt his entire body flush with fear and shame. He couldn't meet Jesus' eyes. He tried to shrink down so no one would ever find him again.

"I know what you think of the boys who help out around here, and I'm glad you never acted on those urges. I'm impressed with your strength. You probably could have gotten away with it, and I'm grateful that you knew how wrong it would have been. Very few in your position would have been able to resist."

"I'm sorry, Lord," Potts said. He clasped his

hands together, as if in prayer. "I—"

"Let me unburden you," Jesus said. Gently, he touched Potts's chest, directly over his heart, and the hole in his wrist filled with light.

When Jesus pulled back, Potts felt like a heavy weight had been lifted from him. With shock he realized he no longer felt the desire that had been plaguing him for the past ten years.

"Thank you, Jesus!" he cried out.

"Some people don't just need physical healing," Jesus said. "I'm here to heal everyone in *all* ways, to make them as strong as they can possibly be. Do you understand?"

Potts sobbed, resisting the sudden need to drop to his knees again. "Yes. Yes, I understand."

Jesus plucked a few sheets of Kleenex from a box on the reverend's desk and offered them to him. Potts took them and started sopping at his eyes and nose. Jesus said, "Good. Let's get to work."

It took everyone a long time to get Potts's flock together, but before long the church bustled with activity, mostly of the elderly variety since it was a work day. Joe watched as the room flooded with people, and he wondered how Jesus would get to everyone. He also wondered how they would get past the original doubt—the one he, himself, had felt upon meeting Jesus for the first time—but he knew the power of faith.

After the coming flow of people slowed down, and there was standing room only,

Potts took to the pulpit, beaming with the confidence of a man who has just been rewarded for a lifetime of blind belief.

He adjusted the microphone. "Thank you all for coming today. I have come to you bearing the greatest news you will ever likely receive in your life. Certainly the best you've gotten so far."

He glanced over to Jesus, who gave him an encouraging thumbs-up. Potts said, "He's back, folks. Jesus Christ has returned to us in our darkest hour. And he's here to help us all."

Joe expected a cacophony of shocked cries, and while he still heard a few doubtful voices, he instead got a majority of people cheering. Instant faith. He'd forgotten what that was like.

"Some of you may think I speak figuratively, but I assure you Jesus is literally here. In our presence. He chose to come back to us, to this community, first. Ladies and gentlemen, I give you our Lord and savior, Jesus Christ!"

Jesus walked to the center of the room. Potts came down from the pulpit, but Jesus did not ascend. Instead he stood with the flock, appraising their expectant faces. No one uttered a word. They waited in silence.

"Hi," he said. "I'm Jesus. Good to see you all."

No one knew what to say. They stared back at him, wide-eyed.

"I see there are a lot of people here who have seen better times," Jesus said. "Many of you get around with canes and walkers. Some of you can barely hear me because of the hearing aids you wear. Some of you can barely see me because your glasses are so thick. I sense a lot of cancer here, too. I have great news, though. All of that ends today."

The parishioners glanced at each other, uncertain. Confused. Some were even scared.

"I want you all to join hands," Jesus said. "Go on. Grab the hand of the person next to you. Those of you on the end of the pews, reach behind you and hold hands with the person back there. Make it so that we all make one zigzagged chain, all the way to the back."

People started murmuring, but they all knew each other. No one had a problem following instructions. Soon, each and every person in the church was linked with everyone else, making one large circle that began and ended where Jesus stood in front of the flock.

"Everyone, be cool," he said. "This might seem odd at first, but I promise you that you'll feel better than you have in years. Some of you, in decades."

He reached out a hand to each side of the room, and when those parishioners took them, the circuit was complete. His hair started perking up, and his eyes glowed. His hands emitted light, and the entire room gasped as one.

Joe looked away, but the power flowing from Jesus was overpowering. Brighter than ever, the room went completely white. The force of it lifted Jesus off his feet until he levitated, tethered to the ground only by those who held him. One by one, their heads blazed to life, and Joe felt himself go blind. He clapped his hands over his eyes, and he could still see the Lord's healing light, bright as day.

And then it dissipated. The photographic burn faded from his retinas, and he could see once again. Jesus dropped to his knees, but no one seemed to notice. Those who had gone bald now had full heads of hair. Those who'd gone gray now shone vibrantly with the original color of their hair. Cataracts vanished, skin tightened, joints once weak grew strong. Withered muscles bunched up in strong pillars. People who had trouble standing up out of chairs now sprang to their feet.

Laughter filled the room. People who had been seventy now looked thirty, and they all jumped about with glee. One man who had been gnarled with arthritis actually did a cartwheel.

And then came the great discarding. A pile formed in the middle of the room. Glasses, hearing aids, crutches, walkers, canes, dental bridges, everything.

And Jesus smiled. He couldn't help it.

CHAPTER 3:
CALLING HOME

Word spread quickly. Rev. Potts brought Jesus around to all the hospitals in the area, to the other churches, and he spent the rest of the day healing those who needed it and bringing youthful vigor back to those who had lost it. And all the while, everywhere he went, people flocked to him, begging for him to cure their glaucoma, their shingles; everything from cancer to hangnails. He did it all without a second thought.

But, even he couldn't keep going forever. He wore out near nightfall and asked Joe to bring him home. "Don't worry, folks," Jesus said to all. "I'll be back tomorrow. I'll get to everyone, I promise."

"You've done plenty today," Potts said. "Thank you."

Joe and his family piled into the Plymouth, and Jesus rode shotgun. Unsurprisingly, a column of vehicles followed them as they drove back to the MacDonald farm.

Joe didn't seem to notice. "That was amazing, Jesus. I can't believe this is really

41

happening. Reverend Potts is just ecstatic. I've never seen him so thrilled. You're really going to change things, Jesus. Forever."

His voice trembled with joy, and he couldn't stop talking. "He's got huge plans for you. He told me that he was going to put out the word right away. You're going to be on the TV this time tomorrow."

He twisted around in his seat so he could look at his wife. "What do you think of that, honey? We're going to be on the TV!"

"Joe!" Ursula said. "Watch the road!"

He turned back, front and center. "Reverend Potts is going to contact everyone he knows in the church. We're going to have people coming from all over the world to be healed. If things work out, they might even send the President of the United States out to meet us! We're going to be famous!"

Ursula couldn't stand the constant jabber coming from her husband. She also felt nervous about the motorcade following them. She leaned forward, touching Joe's shoulder. "We're being followed."

"Don't let that worry you," Joe said. "They just want to see the miracle maker with their own eyes."

They turned down the dirt path that led to their house. Already they could see people setting up camp in their front yard. They kept a respectful distance, but that didn't mean they weren't trespassing. It looked like they were in for the long haul; many had erected tents and lean-tos. Campfires, safely confined by circles of stones, blazed, and people cooked their dinners.

If this had happened before yesterday, Joe would have run everyone off with a shotgun. He didn't like to use his weapon like that, but he wouldn't have tolerated such behavior. Generally, he liked to be private.

But Jesus had changed everything. Joe wanted to share the savior with everyone, and he didn't mind the fame that would bring. In fact, something he'd never recognized within himself bloomed like a weed: a desire for celebrity. Sometimes he watched the reality shows on the History Channel, and he thought he'd do a good job on one of those. Ursula swore to him that they were all phony, and that the people involved were actors, but Joe knew better. He'd been a life-long redneck, and he knew his own kind.

Now? He'd be on the news for sure. Hollywood would probably want to buy his story. His heart suddenly froze when he realized that he would probably be on Bill O'Reilly's show. He tried to think of what that would be like, and he just couldn't. Joe didn't think of himself as easily star-struck. He'd met one of the Dukes of Hazzard once, and he hadn't been very impressed. But Bill O'Reilly was one of the greatest Americans currently walking the earth. Could Joe manage to keep it together in such an august presence?

He parked the car, and everyone filed out. The crowd gathered around, but they still kept their distance. No one said a word as all eyes watched Jesus stretch and get out of the car. Ethan and Allen looked at their audience, eyes wide and shocked. Neither of them had seen anything like it, and they felt a sense of stage fright, like the teacher had just asked them to deliver a speech to the entire school.

Ursula saw this and put her hands on their backs. "Come on, kids. It's dinner time." She ushered them to the house, and they walked in the eerie silence.

Joe walked with Jesus, keeping up his constant chatter. "It's going to be a media circus, Jesus. I hope you have the energy for that." Then he laughed, slapping his forehead. "Heck. What am I thinking? You're the son of God. Of course you have the energy."

"Actually, I'm feeling kind of tired," Jesus said. "Would you be offended if I lay down for a while? Undisturbed?"

They stepped into the house after Ursula and the kids. Bewildered, Joe shook his head. "Offended? No sir. You can do no wrong, my friend. Go on. We won't bother you."

Jesus turned his head back and forth, rubbing his neck. "Could you please get me a glass of water?"

"Sure," Joe said. "Hey Ursula, could you get Jesus a glass please?"

She nodded and went to fetch it.

"You sure you don't want dinner?" Joe asked. "Ursula's making steak and potatoes. She's a mighty fine cook."

"No thank you," Jesus said. "It's been a long day. Tomorrow's probably going to be longer."

Ursula returned with a tall glass filled

almost to the brim with water. She handed it to Jesus. He said, "Thank you. Goodnight."

Joe and Ursula watched him walk up the stairs, up to their bedroom. When they heard the door close, Joe turned to her. "Well, I have a few chores to see to before we eat."

"Chores?" she said.

"I know. It seems strange that after the day we've had, I'm going to do something as regular as chores. But there you go."

"You'd better change your clothes. I don't want you to ruin your good duds."

Annoyed, his mouth tightened. "I know. I know."

Upstairs, Jesus set the glass of water down on the night table and sat on the bed. He looked at the liquid for a while, and then he waved a hand over it. It darkened immediately to a fine red, and he could smell wine. He contemplated this for a while, and then waved his hand over it again. This time it turned into a rich amber color, and the acrid odor of whiskey filled his nostrils.

Nodding, he took down half of the glass in one go. The warmth hit him immediately, and his shoulders no longer seemed so stiff. The world around him softened, and he leaned back, resting on the headboard.

With a sigh he held both hands up at chest level, and he closed his eyes. The holes in his wrists glowed, and something shimmered in his palms. Unlike when he healed people, though, this turned a sickly green that illuminated his face, making him look like a corpse.

45

The amorphous glow took shape. It remained vague, but it took on the slight shape of a humanoid face with holes for eyes and a mouth. Jesus looked at it, waiting.

A mechanical voice sounded: "Progress report."

"I arrived safely," Jesus said. "The process of subjugation has begun. They completely believe I'm Jesus Christ."

"Good. How soon before we can take their planet?"

Jesus chewed the inside of his cheek for a moment, his lips pursed. "I might need some time. Things move slowly around here, and there are a lot of humans. If I work at it like a motherfucker, I should say earth will be ours by the end of their annual cycle."

The voice chuckled, and as vague as the head seemed, a very obvious sneer took shape. "I don't know why you do things this way. You should just crush these insects. Put the fear in them."

"You catch more flies with honey," Jesus said.

"It's better to be feared than loved."

"I see you've been boning up on earth lore."

"If I'm going to rule their world, I should know what they're like."

"True. But remember: if you make them fear you, they will constantly want to rebel against you. They will view you as an enemy. If we do things my way, we will have a loyal army at our beck and call. Wouldn't that be preferable?"

The voice seemed to spit. "They're

weaklings. Fuck them."

"They're stronger than they seem. Plus, since I've been healing them and making them younger, they have stronger backs. The better for us, you know."

The voice remained silent for a moment. Then: "Fine. We'll do it your way. Don't fuck it up like you did on—"

"I don't need to be reminded of my failings. It won't happen again."

The head nodded. "Keep me in the loop."

"Understood."

The head dissipated, and the light flowed back into Jesus' wrists. He dropped his hands into his lap and closed his eyes again. He drew in a deep breath and let it whoosh out of him. Then he took up the glass of whiskey and downed the rest of it. Ran his hand over it again. The droplets at the bottom turned back to water. Couldn't be too careful. Ursula would probably clean the glass later, and Jesus didn't think she'd understand a savior who drank hard liquor.

He molted out of his clothes and slipped under the covers. It didn't take long for him to drift off.

CHAPTER 4:
THE FIRST INTERVIEWS

For the second day in a row Jesus woke up to a loud pounding on his door. Grimacing, he dragged himself out of bed. The room felt a bit distant, and he swayed a little, off balance. He remembered the tall drink last night and turned the last remnants of alcohol in his body back into water. His perception snapped back into place right away, and he stretched, energized and ready to face the day.

He opened the door and saw Joe. "What's up?"

"Late riser, eh?" Joe asked.

Jesus resisted the urge to crack wise about sleeping for three days straight. "What time is it?"

"Nine. And you've got visitors."

"Already?"

"Reverend Potts sent them over," Joe said. "They're reporters from the local stations. A few print journalists are there, too. They want to talk to you."

Jesus nodded. "Let me freshen up. I'll be

down soon."

"Here." Joe handed over a bundle of clothes. "Leave the old ones in the hamper, and Ursula will get to them later."

Jesus took the offering. "Wow. I really need to get my own clothes. I can't thank you enough, Joe."

"Just having you here is thanks enough." Joe then turned and went back downstairs.

Jesus took a quick shower and came down to the kitchen. Breakfast had already come and gone, but Ursula had saved some bacon and eggs for him. He quickly chewed his way through them while Joe chatted with the reporters on the porch. Jesus peered through the window and could see that Rev. Potts was there, too, his collar freshly starched.

Beyond those gathered on the porch, Jesus could see the crowd from last night had grown. People stood or sat closely together, almost all the way back to the road. More than a few people in wheelchairs had shown up.

He washed the food down with some milk and went out the front door. Joe brightened when he saw Jesus and waved. "Gentlemen, here he is. The man himself."

The reporters—there were five of them—started to approach, but one of them took the lead. He wore his hair back with enough product in it to form an impenetrable helmet. His flawless skin stretched over a lean frame, and his teeth flashed brightly enough that he could have been chewing on a lamp.

"Sorry, boys," he said to the others. "The

good reverend gave me the exclusive. You'll have to wait your turn."

The others seemed to want to argue, but none of them said anything. Jesus peeked into the first reporter's mind and saw that he was the top dog in this town. No one wanted to mess with him.

"Hi," the reporter said. "My name is—"

"Antonio Santana," Jesus said. "I know."

Antonio chuckled. "I didn't know they got the channel seven news in Heaven."

"We get it all, Antonio. Even the premium movie channels."

The reporters all broke out into laughter. Antonio smiled. "Cute. Listen, I have my camera guy setting up for the interview over on this side of the house. The lighting is perfect over there. We're going to go live in about five minutes. It's network TV, so keep it clean. And—"

"Come on," Joe said. "He's Jesus. He doesn't curse."

Antonio looked at him as if he thought Joe was an idiot. "Right. Anyway, I'll just ask a few questions, we'll get a few laughs, and then we'll turn it back to the studio so Jack can give everyone the weather for the umpteenth goddamn time."

Joe grimaced when he heard the blasphemy, but he didn't say anything.

Neither did Jesus.

"It's going to be a fluff piece, so don't get all nervous. But if I find out you stutter, I'm cutting this thing short. No one wants to suffer through that. Okay?"

Jesus offered a tolerant smile. "It sounds like you don't believe I am who I say I am, Antonio."

Antonio tried to wither him with a glance. "Don't give me that shit. I think you're funny, and I can see a bit of charm in you, but you'll be forgotten as soon as Trevor Noah does a bit on you. If you're lucky, you'll be a meme."

Jesus nodded. "Okay."

They went around the corner and over to where the cameraman worked at setting up the shot. Antonio picked up a microphone and took a quick look into a small shaving mirror. One more check for food in his teeth, and he walked into the path of the camera.

"His face good?" he asked. "Do we need makeup?"

The cameraman—Jesus knew his name was Eddie Taft—glanced through the eye piece. "Looks good to me."

Antonio plugged something into his ear and started opening his mouth wide over and over again. His lips made strange shapes as he loosened up and got ready to deliver. "How much longer?"

Eddie held up three fingers.

Antonio nodded, listening as the anchors did some stupid cooking bit with a local goof who made cheeseburgers in the shape of a cup for toppings, or whatever. Who gave a shit?

Jesus glanced over to Joe, who stood behind Eddie. Joe's hands wrung together, and he looked very uncomfortable, like a fat guy in a suit just one size too small. Jesus offered a smile, and Joe loosened up.

"All right, get ready," Antonio said. "We're going live in thirty seconds."

A red light clicked on just to the right of the lens, and on a TV behind the camera Joe saw a silent image of the studio. He'd watched this show for years, and he couldn't believe they were about to shoot a story at his place. The screen split, and the image of Antonio Santana appeared, close up so that he filled his box.

"Thanks, Tammy," he said. His perfect baritone voice vibrated in Joe's chest. "We're out in the countryside today with a story you're not going to believe. Sir, would you please tell the world who you are?"

The camera shot widened to include Jesus, who stood with his hands clasped in front of his crotch. The microphone went to his mouth. He looked at Antonio, not the camera. "I'm Jesus Christ."

"The son of God?" Antonio sounded like he wanted to laugh, but he kept himself under control.

"That's right."

"And what are you doing out here in the middle of nowhere?"

"I've come back, just like the Bible said. I'm glad I wound up here. I have Joe MacDonald to thank for a lot of things, including a roof over my head."

Antonio didn't seem to be listening. Instead he went straight for the throat. "And why are you back? To save the world?"

"Yes, actually." Now Jesus faced the

camera. "In a manner of speaking. For a long time my followers have had to rely on faith in order to adhere to Christianity. I'm here to change that. I'm here to remove all doubt, to give you the facts. I'm here to heal the world. If you are crippled or diseased in some way, I want to meet you. I can give you back what you've lost: your life. If that's saving the world, then yes, that's why I'm here."

"Come on, you don't really believe you're Jesus."

"I am."

Joe smiled, thinking of the Bible. He wondered if such a reference would be lost on Antonio.

"What would you say to those who think this is a joke in poor taste?" the reporter asked. "That you're mocking their religion?"

"I'd love to talk to people who think that," Jesus said. "Even Joe thought I was crazy, but I changed his mind within the first five minutes of meeting him."

"Oh? If you're actually Jesus Christ, prove it."

Jesus' smile shifted, and Joe thought it looked almost like a wolf's. "Are you sure, Antonio?"

"Yeah. Heal the lame, or walk on a lake, or something."

"How's mind reading work for you?"

"Go for it."

"You've been cheating on your wife of ten years with no less than five women right now, including Tammy back in the studio. Your wife knows, but she tolerates you because you

54

make a lot of money, and she likes being married to someone with your low level of fame. Do you want me to rattle off the names of those other women?"

Antonio snarled and turned to the cameraman. "Cut the feed."

Joe glanced at the TV and saw that Antonio's image had vanished. The anchors stared into the camera, and Tammy looked horrified. Chuck, the male anchor cleared his throat. His mouth moved silently, and it looked like he'd said something about technical difficulties. Joe couldn't read lips, but that one came through pretty clearly.

Antonio got into Jesus' face. "Listen, you son of a bitch. I don't know what kind of game you're playing, but I will cut your nuts off on live television. You will never be interviewed ever again, not by anyone. Not if I can help it."

"Jesus, Tony," Eddie said. "Was he right? Are you banging Tammy?"

"Go fuck yourself." And he threw the mic down, stalking away.

Joe never liked him, and he felt kind of glad that Jesus had humiliated him like that. The other reporters laughed, crowding around Jesus, telling him about what a dickhead everyone thought Antonio was.

A couple of them also worked on TV, but none of them wanted to go with a live interview, not after Antonio had gotten his "exclusive." It wouldn't fly on morning TV, anyway. Still, they taped interviews with him for later. Both treated Jesus with a lot more respect.

But the first one—John Brickman from the local Fox affiliate, who won the right to interview Jesus first by playing rock-paper-scissors with Larry Ellefson from CBS—wanted proof.

"Of course you want proof," Jesus said. "I can't say it enough. That's why I'm here. To eliminate all doubt from your mind."

John chuckled. "I hope you'll not do the mind reading thing with me."

"Don't worry, I only do that to cocky jerks," Jesus said. "I have something much cooler in mind for you. Did you see all of those people out there?" Nodding toward the front of Joe's property.

"It's quite the crowd," John said. "I noticed more than a few of them are suffering from afflictions. There's a rumor making the rounds that you've already healed the sick."

"No rumor, friend. I'm sure Rev. Potts can get you in touch with those I healed."

"That's all well and good, Jesus, but how about a demonstration?"

"Exactly what I was thinking."

They put the recording on pause while Joe went out to find a subject. He came back five minutes later with a fairly sturdy looking man. Short at five-six, his form still looked fairly intimidating. Muscles bristled all over his frame, betraying not an ounce of fat. However, the right side of his face twisted up with mottled scar tissue, and a patch covered up the empty cavern of his eye socket.

The cameraman—not Eddie, but a rat-faced man named Haley Dean—turned the red light back on, and John held his microphone in the newcomer's face. "Please, introduce yourself to the audience."

"I'm Rich Bech."

"I see you're wearing an eye patch. What happened?"

"Iraq. I was a corporal over there. Came home about four years ago after an IED blew up a busload of citizens. Caught some shrapnel and nearly burned my face off. I lost my eye, and it fu—messed with my depth perception, so they couldn't use me. And here I am."

"First of all, thank you for your service," John said. "Would you mind letting the camera get a close up of you?"

The way Rich glanced over to Haley made everyone who saw him realize that yes, he did indeed mind. "Look. I don't believe any of this sh—stuff. I'm only here because my dad's friend's uncle was at that church yesterday. He said this guy healed his arthritis. I had to see this for myself."

Jesus approached the former soldier. "It's okay, son. You never have to wear that eye patch again. You can take it off."

Rich considered this for a moment. He looked Jesus up and down, and then he reached up to his own face. He plucked the patch from over his eye socket, and he turned to the camera, showing a gnarled batch of scar tissue. The pale marks from the stitches could still be seen.

Jesus lifted his hands, and Joe turned

away. No one else knew well enough, but Joe reckoned they soon would. He decided it would be useless to warn them against something like this. The light was something they had to see for themselves.

Haley got it the worst. As the light emanated from Jesus' eyes and mouth, the others squinted against it. John shielded his face with his hand, as if looking into the sun. But Haley had to watch the whole thing to make sure it got recorded. When the glow became brighter than the center of the universe—bright enough to burn the back of his retinas—he screamed. "Fuck!"

No one noticed, and it would later be edited out—as would the sudden turn the camera took—losing focus on the subject. Eddie saw this and knew he had to step in. Ordinarily he wouldn't help another network, but deep in his heart he knew the scene unfolding before him was one of the most important things he could ever record. He grabbed the camera and straightened it out, looking at Jesus' feet instead and guessing where his head was.

The light abated, and Eddie risked a glance into the eyepiece. His guess had been right—thankfully—and Jesus moved out of the way, showing off a brand new Rich Bech. Not only did the flesh on the right side of his face gleam like a newborn's, but the ugly tissue had cleared away and a new eye had bloomed in its place.

Rich blinked, and he looked at his hand, opening and closing each eye one at a time.

Finally he looked back to Jesus, and tears cut tracks down his cheeks. "Thank you. I . . . this . . . it's not possible. But it happened. Thank you!"

Savagely, he threw the eye patch to the ground and stomped on it. Then he remembered where he was, and he picked it up again, not wanting to litter on someone else's property.

John and Larry gaped at Jesus, and two men who made their living from talking found they couldn't speak. They didn't even know what they could say. Slowly, John's head pivoted toward the camera. He didn't even notice the man behind it. "Please tell me you got that."

"Fuckin-A right I did," Eddie said.

"It can't be real," Larry said. "It was makeup or something. Rich is a plant. Right?"

Jesus rolled up his sleeves and showed both sides of his hands like a magician. "I've got more where that came from."

"Hold on a sec," Eddie said. He ran back to the news van and came back sporting a pair of shades. "Okay, let's do this."

Just like the previous day at the church, Joe and Rev. Potts coordinated in order to get everyone lined up and ready to be healed. Before long Eddie, Haley and Larry's cameraman—a pasty-faced kid by the name of Dave—videoed Jesus as he went down the line, healing diseases, growing missing limbs, curing osteoporosis and restoring lost senses. Again, a pile of crutches and other assorted aids piled up, and Rich promised Joe that he'd cart it all away himself.

"Don't want your yard all cluttered up," he said.

Larry conducted his own interview, and soon the print journalists had their turn. As all of this happened the crowd grew even bigger, and more people showed up to be cured. Jesus talked as he worked, and more reporters showed up, inspired by the live footage from earlier. In fact it had gone viral. Buzzfeed already had the story, and Fark had already made fun of it.

The house phone rang off the hook. Every national news network wanted a piece of Jesus. William Morris wanted to represent him. Jimmy Kimmel wanted to bump Robert DeNiro if Jesus would do his show that very night.

Ursula finally gave up trying to answer it, so she pulled the plug. They didn't have cell phones—they give you cancer, you know—so she didn't have to worry about them getting a hold of them any other way, unless they wanted to try snail mail.

A helicopter flew overhead. News vans lined up down the dirt road leading to the street. Cameras grew like weeds.

During that second interview, the one with John Brickman, Joe had thought this whole adventure to be grand. Exciting. Now? It was turning into a nightmare. The yard was being torn to pieces by this much traffic. Not to mention all the garbage that would be left behind. He couldn't depend on Rich alone to clean all that up. That would be unfair. Not to mention that some of the people who had stayed overnight had gone to the bathroom out in the open.

He never thought it would be like this. But he held his silence. This was too important to the world.

That night, he would have to chase off a TMZ reporter who tried to take a picture of Jesus through the curtained bedroom window. The following night, he caught some kid trying to spray paint anti-Christian graffiti on the back of his house. That morning someone showed up with a gun, wanting to sacrifice Jesus again. Luckily, Joe's shotgun was much bigger and much scarier.

But, the day after that? Joe cheered up for that one. Jesus was going on Brian Murphy's show.

CHAPTER 5:
THE NO BS ROOM

Joe would have preferred Bill O'Reilly, but it would seem the Fox star wasn't interested in interviewing the Lord and savior. Sean Hannity also showed a remarkable lack of interest. They couldn't even get Glenn Beck.

But, they did get Brian Murphy, and that wasn't half-bad. Joe liked his show. It ripped off the Factor a bit, and Murphy came off as a pale shadow of O'Reilly, but he still spouted his opinions on a Fox News show, which he called The No BS Room. Joe admired him a good deal.

The network flew Jesus in to New York, where Murphy filmed his show. They set him up in a five-star hotel and gave him an expense account and a hefty check. The royal treatment. At first, Jesus didn't want to do it that way. He said he would take a Greyhound to the city, and he'd stay in a no-tell. Fox would have none of it.

"In that case," Jesus said over the phone, "I have a small request."

"Name it," the network rep said.

"I want Joe MacDonald to come with me."

Joe, who stood in the corner of the kitchen, sipping coffee and listening to the conversation, gave him a glance. He didn't care to leave the farm or his family behind, even if it was only for a brief trip to New York.

"Done," the rep said.

"Cool."

After Jesus hung up, Joe said, "I don't know about that. Ursula and the kids need me, what with all this mess outside." He waved a hand toward the window, through which they could both see a gaggle of people, most of which kept at a goodly distance. Some of them did their best to get a peek at the savior.

"You have to come, Joe. You're my right-hand man."

Right-hand man? A shudder went through Joe's body. He recalled that Jesus supposedly sat at the right hand of God, while Satan stood at the left, which was why left-handed people were looked askance upon. In Latin the word for right is "dexter." The word for left? "Sinister." To imagine that he stood at Jesus' right? He couldn't breathe for a moment.

"I need you," Jesus continued. "I can't do this alone. I want you to be my earthly representative. You've got your head on right. More importantly, when I healed you, I didn't have to take any terrible thoughts or urges out of you. You're pure of heart."

Joe actually blushed at this, and he looked away. He found an ant on the kitchen floor, and he watched it trundle its way across the linoleum. "I . . . I'm not worthy."

"Of course you are. Look at your life. You have a wonderful family, and you own everything you have without owing anyone else. My father didn't make many like you, Joe. That's why I need you. Will you join me? Please?"

Joe tore his gaze away from the ant and looked into Jesus' vivid brown eyes. "What about Ursula? I can't leave her alone, not with that crowd."

"Rich will take care of it," Jesus said. "I'll bet he'll be all too happy."

Rich Bech had been around a lot lately. He'd taken it upon himself to provide security for the MacDonald farm. "If you want these people out of here, say the word," he'd told Joe. He'd also taken to patrolling at night, especially after the incident with the spray paint.

"Okay," Joe said. "If Rich will stick around, I'll go with you."

Jesus grinned. "Thanks, Joe. Now, do you have access to email? Fox said they'd send us the flight and booking info that way."

Joe didn't even understand the internet, so with some help from Eddie Taft—who had also taken it upon himself to stick around, helping out whenever he could—they got Joe a Gmail account, called Fox back with the address and managed to print up the itinerary.

That very night they headed out to the airport, driven in a limo also supplied by Fox. Joe had never been inside one, nor had he ever cared to be. It always struck him as a bit excessive. You didn't need something like this to get around unless you were showing off for those folks less fortunate. What was wrong with a regular car? Just so long as it got you from point A to point B, that should be good enough, right?

But he found himself enjoying the ride. Surprised, he noticed a bar in the back. Not that he drank. The only alcohol he'd ever had —aside from sacramental wine on Sundays— was when he'd been in high school doing stupid teenager stuff.

The bar did have water, though. Grateful, he took a bottle and drank deeply.

Joe had never been on a plane before, either. This scared him, a bit. Most people wouldn't think twice of strapping themselves into a large metal object and exploding a fair amount of fuel to shoot themselves into the sky, but it didn't sit well with him. Suddenly, he thought maybe a drink would have calmed his nerves a bit.

Very few people onboard gawked at Jesus. Maybe because he wasn't famous enough yet. That would change very soon.

When the plane took off Joe gripped the armrests and refused to look out the window. His stomach lurched, and he thought the roar of the engines was really some kind of explosion. Something had to be wrong with the plane.

"Relax," Jesus said. "You're with me."

Logically Joe knew he should have unwound a bit at that. Still, he couldn't help it. He didn't muster the courage to lift the window cover until the plane had leveled out and the seat belt light went off. When he saw the thick cotton carpet beneath them, he couldn't believe that what he saw below was the rest of the world.

Landing went a bit better. His ears popped too much, and he felt sick, but he no longer feared for his life. Besides, the city lights in the growing dusk were actually beautiful. He'd seen nothing like it before.

A limo took them to their hotel. Joe had seen places like this in movies, but he never expected to stay in one. The view of the city nearly floored him. The stocked fridge couldn't have been meant for them, could it? Again he found alcohol—complimentary—but he didn't partake.

They got dressed up in suits. Joe still had the one he wore when he graduated from high school. Just a week ago, he wouldn't have fit in it. Now, he filled it perfectly. Not too big, not too small. Like baby bear's porridge, it was just right.

Jesus looked strange in his suit with his hair tied back in a ponytail and his beard trimmed and neat. He looked like a polished bum. Not that Joe would ever say that, of course. But, still.

Another limo picked them up from the hotel and took them to the studio, where the rep—a slick looking young man named Travis

Welter—met them at the guest door with a hearty handshake.

"Great to meet you, Jesus," he said. "Flight good?"

"As good as a flight can be, I guess," Jesus said. As if he'd been in a plane before and had plenty of experience.

"Everything meet your expectations?"

"Met and exceeded."

"Good. Good. You must be Joe MacDonald."

Joe shook hands with him, too. "That's me."

"Okay, we're heading up to the green room. That's where you'll wait, Joe. Jesus, you'll come with me to makeup, and we'll get you locked and loaded and ready for TV."

"Sounds good."

The green room. Joe had heard of such places, and he'd always imagined a grungy place with a dirty couch and an equally dirty table, which would be covered with day-old food. What he got was much different. The ambiance radiated soothing calmness, and the table was fully stocked with fresh food. A television dominated one wall, so everyone could watch the live program. At the time, no one else sat with Joe, which he didn't mind. He supposed this room usually contained big names, and he didn't know how he would respond if he ran into, say, Dennis Miller for example.

Out in the studio, the audience settled into their seats and waited for the show to begin. Lights on the set already blazed, and the crew crawled all over the place getting everything ready.

In the makeup room Jesus sat side by side with Brian Murphy while young women powdered their faces.

"So you're the guy, huh?" Murphy asked.

"That's me."

"You're really serious with all this shit?" Murphy waved a hand at Jesus, up and down.

"Of course. By the way I had my friend, Eddie, send you that footage you're going to want to play tonight."

Murphy didn't seem to have heard him. "Listen. I'm a reasonable man and a responsible broadcaster. I just want to remind you that you're going to be in the No BS Room. I'm not kidding with that title, Jesus. All right?"

"Okay."

Murphy whipped off the towel around his neck and dropped it on the floor, where one of the makeup girls picked it up. Not that he noticed. "See you out there," he told Jesus.

When Jesus' makeup was done, the PD rushed over and led him to the wings, where he would wait until Murphy started his Jesus segment.

In the green room Joe watched the No BS Room. Murphy spouted off on a few things in the news. He criticized the president for wanting more gun laws. He congratulated a pastor in Oklahoma for insisting that the schools in his area had a five-minute prayer session before classes began. He tore George Clooney apart for spreading the liberal agenda in regards to greenhouse gases, which probably didn't really exist anyway. No scientist had ever proved it, had they?

Joe nodded in agreement. Murphy was on fire tonight.

"All right, I've had enough of this Clooney guy. Who does he think he is? If he's got something to say, he's welcome to come on my show and defend himself. We've reached out to his agent, and of course we've gotten no response." The camera paused meaningfully on his face.

Another camera took over, and he turned his head to face it. "When we come back from break, we have a story you won't believe. Depending on your world viewpoint, this could be either good news or bad news. You decide. Jesus Christ is next."

It cut to commercial, and Joe made a sandwich from the cold cuts and bread on the table. He suffered through two and a half minutes of sentimental car commercials, pseudo-humorous phone ads and party booze garbage before the No BS Room came back on.

In the studio the cameraman gave Murphy the cue, and he smiled. "Welcome back to the No BS Room, folks. Tonight our guest is very unusual. He's stirred a lot of controversy, and I'm glad to have him on so we can hash this whole thing out. Believe him or not, he says he's the Lord and savior, Jesus Christ himself. Hello, Jesus."

"Thanks for having me on your show, Brian," Jesus said.

"Listen. This is the No BS Room. We don't tolerate liars and the lies they tell. So let's get down to it. You're Jesus Christ, right? As in, the son of God. Nazareth and Legion and the crucifixion and all of that?"

"That's me." The grin he wore on his face almost seemed goofy, like he knew Murphy thought this was a fluff piece.

"There's a question on all of our minds, Jesus. This is very important. I've wanted to ask you this for a long time. Are you a Republican or a Democrat?"

"My answer's not going to be a popular one, Brian."

"Oh no. You're a Democrat." A playful smile twitched on his face. The audience laughed.

"It doesn't matter, actually. Change is coming, and that will be a moot question. My return marks the end of all conflict, both physical and political."

"Now wait a minute. You mean to tell me that you're going to change the bipartisan system we have in this country?"

"In the world. Democrat or Republican? It won't matter. Christian or Muslim? It won't matter. Rich or poor? It won't matter. Black or white? It won't matter. What will matter? Love. We will all be one. No more borders. It's going to be heaven on earth, Brian."

"Didn't we try this in the 'Sixties? I'm sorry, Jesus, but the world will not tolerate that hippie crap. Do you really have that kind of faith in humanity?"

"Faith is on the way out, Brian. I'm here to

give you all the answers you've ever prayed for. Knowledge changes a lot of things. You won't have to wonder about anything anymore. There will be *one* ideology because there will be *no* room for doubt. As soon as everyone in the world knows everything, love will set them free from their own shackles."

Murphy feigned shock. "Shackles? What are you talking about? Our philosophies drive us. They make us powerful. This is the No BS Room, and I'm calling you out, Jesus."

The audience clapped and hooted. In the green room Joe felt his heart shrink. He'd expected doubt from a guy like Murphy, but nothing like this. If this kept up, he'd wipe the walls with Jesus. Joe panicked, wondering if he should go out there and help. Maybe they should show the video. That would change things.

On the screen Jesus only smiled indulgently. "How strongly do you believe in your philosophy, Brian?"

"Wholeheartedly." Murphy waved his hand around the studio. "My belief is so powerful it got me this sweet job and all of these wonderful supporters."

Again the crowd cheered.

"Then why'd you change them early in your career?" Jesus asked.

"What do you mean?"

"Before you became a big name, you were a registered Democrat. But when your AM talk show crashed and burned, you switched parties. You modeled your new self after Republican pundits almost to the point of parody, and here you are, the third most popular host on Fox News. Here's the biggest thing that surprises me, though: you've told your lies so often that you actually believe them now. *That* is the power of belief. And I'm here to change that."

The crowd went dead silent. Joe stared at the screen, unbelieving. Could this be true? Why would Jesus lie about something like this? He noticed Murphy had gone pale—well, paler than usual—and his lips twitched, flummoxed.

For a moment Joe thought this would be a repeat of the Antonio Santana incident, but then Murphy's face snapped back into shape. His eyes glittered, and his smile turned into a wolf's grin.

"Okay. We'll play it that way. No more BS from you. I want you to prove you're the real Jesus Christ right here. Right now. I want a miracle performed on live television."

"Weren't the ones I did for the local affiliates good enough for you?" Jesus asked. It felt to Joe like Jesus was setting up a trap of some kind. He didn't know why he got that impression, but he couldn't help it.

"Come on. I'm pretty sure I saw Criss Angel heal the crippled on one of his shows. Maybe he's the real Jesus. What do you think of that?"

"Okay, name a miracle. I'll do it."

"Let's start simple." Murphy held up his mug. "I have water in here. Turn it into wine."

Jesus pulled back the sleeve on one arm,

showing both sides of his hand. The lights made a shadow in the hole on his wrist. Then, he waved a hand over Murphy's mug. "Go ahead. Give it a taste."

Murphy stared at him for a moment, and it became clear to Joe that the host hadn't expected Jesus to do anything. Doubt seeped onto his face for the first time, but he lifted the mug to his lips and drank. His eyes widened, and he spat the liquid out.

It came out thick and red.

"I made it a bit stronger than usual," Jesus said. "So you can taste the alcohol. I know you're a big drinker."

Murphy, flabbergasted, wiped the wine from his quivering lips. "BS. This is BS. Some kind of magic trick. I don't know how you did it, but I know you did something."

Jesus leaned in. "Then let's stop messing around. Ask me for the miracle you really want to see."

"I want you to cure some cripples," Murphy said.

Behind the camera, the director panicked at the politically incorrect language. He tried to get Murphy's attention, drawing a finger across his throat, but the host ignored him.

"Not just any cripples, either," he continued. "Anyone can do that. Televangelists do it all the time. No, I want you to heal someone I know. Someone famous. Like, Michael J. Fox or someone."

"Ask and you shall receive," Jesus said. He turned to the director and twirled his finger in a circle. "Roll the tape, if you please."

The camera cut away so they could play the video Eddie had sent them. It also ran from a TV screen off-camera. Murphy watched as a vibrant young man ran down a path with a giant, toothy grin.

"I don't get it," Murphy said. "Who is this?"

"I know it's hard to recognize him without the wheelchair and the glasses, but that's Stephen Hawking."

"Bullshit."

The director once again waved furiously, and Murphy pointed at him. "Stop doing that, you fucking epileptic." He turned back to Jesus. "That is not Stephen Hawking. You are a liar and this is a lie."

"Is your doubt that strong?" Jesus asked.

"Of course. I have no tolerance for morons."

"How about your knee? The one you—"

"Everyone knows about that. I caught some shrapnel in Vietnam."

Jesus rolled his eyes. "For a show called the No BS Room, there seems to be a lot of BS being flung around."

Murphy's face tightened, and Joe thought he could see fear in his eyes.

"Why don't you tell your fans how you really got the bum knee?"

Murphy stared at Jesus, afraid to so much as speak.

"You were in the army, sure," Jesus said. "But you never saw action. The war ended before you got out of boo—"

"How could you know that?" Murphy whispered. In the rapt silence it sounded like a car alarm going off. "No one knows. Do you know how much money I paid to seal those records?"

"Yes, actually," Jesus said. "I *do* know. And I also know that you dropped your gun and it went off, getting you in the knee."

Murphy stuttered, locked into a downward spiral. His face kept changing colors, from white to red and back again. He almost blubbered.

"Relax," Jesus said. "I'm not here to humiliate you. I'm here to help." And he reached out for Murphy's head with both hands.

Murphy flinched, but he didn't back away. He looked like his insides had all been scooped out, and all that held him up in his chair was his skin. Then Jesus began to glow, and Joe looked away.

Had he kept watching, he would have seen the screen go so bright that it pixilated and flickered, nearly shutting down. He heard the audience gasp, but whether it was from the light or the miracle, Joe didn't know. When he finally looked back he saw Murphy standing up behind his desk, squatting up and down. Then he held one leg up and worked the hinge of his knee.

Come to think of it, his balding head now sported a full sprout of thick, dark hair.

"That can't be," he said.

Jesus shrugged.

"This knee has bugged me every day since the 'Seventies. Even with painkillers, I can always feel a faint ache."

Jesus waited.

Murphy looked at him. "You healed me."

This time Jesus smiled.

Murphy dropped to both knees without so much as a wince and bowed before Jesus. "I can't believe I called you a liar. I cursed in front of you. I . . . I . . ."

Jesus pulled him up to his feet. "It's okay, Brian. I forgive you."

Then, shocker of all shocks, Brian Murphy wept openly on national television, something he'd only done once before, when the Twin Towers fell on 9/11.

Jesus turned to the crowd. "Now that we've got that out of the way, who's in need of being healed?"

Everyone instantly stood up and rushed down the stairs as one. Security guards jumped in to hold them back until they could be organized.

"We need to go to break," the director said.

"No, we don't," Murphy said. "Don't you dare."

"But the sponsors—"

"Fuck 'em. This is more important."

"More important than the sponsors?" The director stared at him, aghast.

"You heard me. Don't you miss a second of this."

Joe watched from the green room as Jesus walked down the line of audience members, touching them and healing them. Turning back their clocks. Renewing their sense of wonder. It brought a tear to his eye. Sometimes he couldn't believe this was really happening. His mind had a perverse desire to snap back to the way things were before Jesus returned. This had to be some kind of fantasy. Maybe he'd fallen and hit his head on a rock, and his coma-bound brain produced this wonderful dream to ease his way into the next world.

And then he held strong, knowing in his heart of hearts that this was real. Jesus had truly come back, and the world would be healed forever.

The program ran over, and no one seemed to care. Sean Hannity, who had a show on after Murphy, arrived in a huff, but when Jesus touched him he changed. He knelt before the Lord and savior, like everyone else, and just like with everyone else Jesus pulled him back to his feet.

Once everyone had taken their turn Jesus settled back at the desk with Murphy, and he turned more water into wine. Drinking, Murphy continued the interview, begging to ask more questions.

"Knock yourself out," Jesus said. "That's what I'm here for."

First: "What are your thoughts on gay marriage?"

"The very idea of marriage—straight or gay—is disgusting to my father. It's not about love. It's about business. If you love someone, you don't need to sign a contract. But I don't think that's what you meant with your question. You're wondering if homosexuality is a sin."

"Well . . ."

"Absolutely not. Love is the most important thing in the universe, and reproduction has nothing to do with that."

The crowd, most of whom would probably have lynched Jesus earlier today, actually cheered. It made Joe feel a bit uncomfortable, since he didn't think a man should lay with a man, but, well, the Lord had just said it was okay. Who was he to doubt the Lord?

"ASK HIM ABOUT SCHOOL VOUCHERS!" a smart ass from the crowd shouted.

Murphy, whose pet project was the school voucher program, offered an annoyed smile and moved on: "What's your stance on abortion? Is it murder?"

"Yes," Jesus said. "Sorry, liberals, but you got this one wrong. Life does begin at conception. If you can't afford to have a child, then don't have sex."

The audience wasn't as quick to cheer that one. Some of them did. A few more made a good show. But a majority of them couldn't help but think, *What?!*

Joe agreed with the answer.

"Are we descended from monkeys?" Murphy asked.

"Now it's time to apologize to the conservatives," Jesus said. "Yep. Sure are. But why do you think evolution worked? Because it was guided by the hand of God."

Should women be considered equals to men?

"Of course. All people are created equal."

Race?

"It doesn't matter. See my previous statement about love."

Gun control?

"Guns should never have happened," Jesus said. "The price of free will, I suppose. No one should be killing anyone. Therefore, guns shouldn't exist."

"What about not suffering a witch to live?"

"No one should be killing anyone."

"Murders? Pedophiles? Rapists?"

"No one should be killing anyone."

"Let's switch gears. Are you familiar with the Bill of Rights?"

"Sure. I mean, they weren't around the first time I came here, but I studied up before I came back." He winked at the audience, and they laughed now that they knew he was making a joke.

"How many of them do you think your father would agree with?"

The interview continued like this, and Jesus gave answers both comfortable and uncomfortable. Yet even with the latter, everyone decided to let it go. He'd just healed a room full of people. Hell, he'd healed Stephen Hawking. Who could argue with something like that?

By the time the show drew to an end, no doubt remained: the Bible was obsolete. Faith was obsolete. No more speculation: the truth was here. Jesus doled it out as asked, and no one could doubt ever again.

The lights dimmed, and the audience started rushing the stage, desperate for one more contact with Jesus. At the least? An autograph. Security held them at bay as Murphy reached across the desk to shake hands.

"You're the absolute best guest I've ever had on this show," he said. "And I had Ronald Reagan on once."

Jesus shook his hand. "Thanks for helping me spread the word. Without this appearance things would have gone a lot slower for me."

They traded a few more pleasantries and parted ways. A guard led Jesus back to the green room, where he met up with Joe, and they took their limo back to the hotel. During the ride Joe felt overwhelmed. He said, "That was amazing, Jesus."

Jesus leaned his head back and sighed. "It was good. But it wore me out. I can't wait to get into bed tonight."

When they got back to their room Jesus stopped outside the door. He sniffed at the air, and he sensed something crackle around him. He didn't know what it was, but something made him feel a moment of nostalgia, like he'd been transported back to his home for a second.

He turned to Joe. "Listen. Would you mind going down to the lobby for a while? I need to do something, but I have to do it alone."

"Sure," Joe said. He paused, wondering how he should ask his question. Finally he just said, "Do you mind me asking why?"

"I have to talk to my father."

"Oh! I see. Sure, I'll go downstairs."

"I'll call down to the front desk and let you know when it's safe," Jesus said. "People can't look at my father, you know. It's too bright."

Joe nodded and headed for the elevator. Jesus watched him go. When the doors slid shut, Jesus retrieved the hotel room's key and entered. Once inside he ditched his coat and unbuttoned his sleeves, rolling them up his skinny arms. Light already glowed in the holes in his wrists. He could almost smell his flesh cooking.

He held his hands out, palms up, and waited for the face to form. It did, in record time. Within seconds it turned its eyeless visage to him. "Don't bother with the report. I saw the Fox transmission. What is taking you so long?"

"These things take time," Jesus said. "I—"

"Enough. You've played with the humans too much. They need to be subjugated immediately."

"I understand what you need," Jesus said, "but it's not my style. When I'm done with these people, they will do anything you ask, and they will offer no resistance. If I do this the quick way, they'll want to rebel. They'll want to—"

"Who gives a fuck? Let them rebel. We'll just stomp them back into place like we always do."

Jesus tried to force a smile, but it just wouldn't come. "Look, you don't know these people. They're stubborn. If we use force, we might as well just wipe them out. They won't do our bidding based on fear."

This gave the floating head pause. It

hovered above his hands, regarding him with a blank face.

"I said it would be done in a year. The way things have been going, it might even be sooner."

"Make it a month."

"But—"

"No buts. If earth's population isn't enslaved by then, I'll have to make an appearance. *You don't want that.*"

Jesus blanched. "A month then."

"Good. I'll expect a report from you in half that time. The second report will come at the end of the month. If you have failed me . . ."

"I won't."

"Good." The head eased back into his wrist holes, and Jesus rubbed at them, wincing. Maybe his brother was right. This place reminded him of Cava-12, after all, and he didn't want that to happen again. Maybe a good dose of fear would help.

But he didn't want to think about that now. He went to the night table and dialed the front desk. As soon as he'd told Joe he could come up, Jesus didn't wait. He got out of his clothes and into his pajamas before flopping down on his bed.

Downstairs, Joe MacDonald stepped off the elevator and hunted around the lobby for a good place to wait. He found a leather seat near the front desk and settled in. An entertainment magazine lay on the table next to him, so he leafed through it, not reading anything, just looking. He saw a couple of actresses provocatively dressed, and he tsked them under his breath before flipping away from them.

Mel Gibson was making a sequel to *The Passion of the Christ*? How odd. What did he intend to cover, all the epistles? That wouldn't make for much of an interesting movie. Saints writing letters? Ugh. If he decided to go with the Book of Revelation, though . . .

Not that Joe cared for the first movie. He liked the story, but he disapproved of the violence and gore. He also didn't like Satan's appearance. Felt too cheap.

"Excuse me, sir? Hello?"

Joe peered up over the top of the magazine and saw an incredibly beautiful woman standing before him. Long blonde hair tied back into a ponytail, sparkling blue eyes. A sequined green dress sparkling in the lobby lights. It didn't cover much, and he could see a lot of her. More than he would have ordinarily allowed for even on a TV weather lady.

Still, he felt something flutter inside of himself. Maybe a bit under the belt, too. He hadn't felt that in a long time, not even with Ursula. He'd thought that part of his life was over.

"Yes?" he asked.

"Didn't I just see you come in with that guy who was on Fox tonight?"

"Jesus," Joe said. "And yes, I'm with him."

She smiled, showing off a perfect set of teeth. Living out in the boonies, Joe didn't get to see many of those in person. Just on TV. "I thought so. Are you and him friends?"

"I like to think so," Joe said.

She pushed the magazine aside and sat down in his lap, wrapping her arms around his neck. "I would do anything to meet him. *Anything.*"

Joe stiffened and then stiffened again. It had been a long time since he'd felt it go that stiff. His heart beat so savagely he thought it would punch her off his lap. For the first time since he was a teenager, he experienced a sexual thought about someone who wasn't his wife. He imagined bringing this woman upstairs and turning into an animal with her, much like a werewolf with a victim.

Except . . . well, Jesus was up there. If he did that in front of his savior . . .

Heavens. Never mind Jesus. He couldn't do that in a world that contained someone as wonderful as Ursula.

He wilted almost as soon as he'd sprouted. Gingerly he stood, lifting her off his lap and removing her arms from around his neck. "I'm sorry, ma'am. I can't do that. I'm a married man."

Her face reddened, and she looked away from him. "He's not really Jesus though, is he?"

"He is. He healed me."

"I . . . I think I might have had too much to drink tonight," she said.

"Maybe. Perhaps you should pray."

"Maybe I will."

"Excuse me, are you Joe MacDonald?" This from the desk clerk. He held a phone with a hand over the mouthpiece.

"That's me," Joe said.

"Mr. Christ says it's okay to come back up now."

"Thank you."

He turned back to face the young woman, but she'd already left. The doorman had just let her out.

Joe tried not to think about her anymore. He went to the elevator, but as he rode up in silence he couldn't help himself. A certain degree of regret took residence in his heart, especially after what Jesus had said about marriage on the No BS Room. But he couldn't shake his respect for marriage away. He loved Ursula too much.

Maybe he should have invited this woman up so Jesus could cure her of her promiscuity.

Too late now.

He got out of the elevator and approached their room. He slid the key card in place and walked in. Jesus already snored in his bed. From the look of it he'd just dropped down on the mattress, dressed in his pajamas.

Joe took a moment to pull the blanket around Jesus' slumbering form. Tucked it up under his chin. Patted his chest for a moment.

And then he undressed, getting into his own pj's. Bed came shortly after, but sleep didn't catch him for a while longer, that night.

CHAPTER 6: REDISTRIBUTION OF WEALTH

The next morning, Jesus got up first and showered before Joe had even cracked open his eyes. This didn't happen until someone knocked at the door. Jesus, who had just gotten into his clothes for the flight home —a t-shirt and jeans—approached the door. "I'll get it."

Joe jumped up. "No, let me. You never know who it could be."

"Sure I do. It's the manager. He's got some news for us."

Joe started to ask how he knew that, and then he stopped himself when he realized how stupid that would be.

Jesus opened up and the manager stepped in with a black leather folder under his arm. "Mr. Christ, I have a few messages for you."

"Go ahead."

The manager glanced at Joe, who still stood in his pajamas, but he was a professional and looked away immediately. "There are several couriers in the lobby to see you, all from the richest men in the world. And . . . uh . . . Warren Buffett showed up personally. He wants to see you right away."

Warren Buffett? Joe saw him on TV all the time. One of the richest men in the world was down in the lobby, right now, waiting to see Jesus? He started feeling a little star struck.

"Did he show up first?" Jesus asked.

"No. Maybe twentieth. Or so."

"Send him up when it's his turn, then."

Joe stared at Jesus, aghast. He couldn't imagine someone telling a man as rich and powerful as Warren Buffett to wait his turn. Then again he had to remind himself that this was Jesus, not some ordinary friend of his.

Jesus is my friend. Literally.

It nearly floored him.

Jesus and Joe spent the next couple of hours in a whirlwind as guys in suits with briefcases handcuffed to their wrists came up, one by one, and offered their boss's money to Jesus. Each and every one of them said there was more where *that* came from. At first Jesus tried to turn them away but they insisted.

Warren Buffett offered the greatest amount: everything he owned, just for a chance to shake Jesus' hand. He'd liquidated all of his possessions and assets, and it came out to a whopping eighty billion and change.

After fifty more such callers, Joe got impatient. "We really need to get going, Jesus. We're going to miss our flight."

"That's all right. We can catch another."

They spent a half a day accepting monetary

offers from CEOs and presidents and seeing reporters from all around the globe, even a few from Al Jazeera. That last one made Joe nervous but only because of what he remembered from the second Iraq war.

When the final visitor left, it neared dinner time, and Jesus sent for food. "Not that I need any," he said. "But you're looking peckish."

Joe marveled at the mountain of money that had piled up over the course of the day, shocked by how much was there. It had to be billions of dollars. Maybe trillions. Maybe enough to fix the country's deficit. He mentioned this last part, thinking maybe Jesus should use it for that.

"Nah. I got a better use for this." He opened one of the briefcases and withdrew a sheaf of money. There had to be fifty grand in that bundle. He tossed it to Joe. "This is for you."

Joe caught the money and looked down, shocked to see a thousand-dollar bill on top. He could have sworn they didn't make these anymore. Sure enough, the date on it said 1944.

"I can't take this."

"You might as well, Joe. Besides, this paper money isn't going to be worth anything in a week. Might as well take it and spend it while you can. Get something nice for Ursula and the kids."

Joe nodded, thinking about maybe getting a good car for a change. He'd never bought one new, and that would be pretty nice. But then he thought back to the other thing Jesus had said. "What did you mean about this not being worth anything?"

"Just that. I talked to some people last night. Looks like I'm going to the White House in a few days to meet the President of the United States. We have a lot to talk about, and the money system is in the top five. The reason there's such a gap between the poor and the rich is because the rich keep producing these things—" Gesturing to the pile of money and briefcases. "—without having any value to back them up. This paper money isn't real money, it's the idea of money. I'm going to change that, because like our Fox friend, I'm tired of the BS in this world."

"So, what should we do with this stuff, then?" Joe asked. "Burn it?"

"It's still worth something now," Jesus said. "Want to help me get rid of it?"

"How?"

"Do you think you can get on the line with that rep from Fox and see if he can get a group of volunteers together?"

"I could do that."

"Great! Get them to come down here."

An hour later, after Joe had eaten, the troops gathered, and Jesus gave them all a briefcase and marching orders: "Follow me, and we're going to give a bundle of money to every homeless person we see. Whenever we see a soup kitchen, we'll donate. Whenever we find a social service in need, we'll give to them. We'll do this until all of this money is gone."

Everyone merely stared back at him, shocked. No one could process the idea of giving so much cash away, especially to the sort of people who would only spend it on drugs. But then again, this was Jesus. If this was what he wanted . . .

Five minutes into their journey down the streets of New York, all doubt dissipated. People joyously tossed money to complete strangers. It almost seemed cathartic, the way they gave and gave and gave. Some of them didn't even stop with Jesus' money; some of them went into their own wallets. More than a couple offered homeless people the shirts off their backs.

Everyone who received the money also received the touch of Jesus. He cured them all, whether it be physical problems or mental ones. At the end of the day not a single person who took his money spent it on alcohol or heroin or anything else but food. Shelter. Useful supplies.

It was the most beautiful thing Joe had ever seen.

That night Fox splurged on first-class tickets to send Jesus and Joe back home. Upon their arrival they were met by Rich Bech at baggage claim. Out by passenger pick-up, he'd parked his car, and inside waited Joe's family. Together they all headed back to the farm, where the crowd had grown ten times bigger than it had been when Jesus had left.

They cheered when he returned, and he

waved at them all. One by one, he healed them as he went up the walk toward the house. Many begged for a speech, but he told them no. "There will be time enough for speeches. Tomorrow I'm going to meet the president, and I think that's when the speeches will come. Goodnight, everyone!"

The next day the phone rang in the MacDonalds' kitchen. Ursula picked it up with her usual greeting. The voice on the other line said, "Is this Ursula MacDonald?"

Ursula flinched, unused to hearing such authority in a feminine voice. "It sure is."

"This is the president of the United States. I'd like to speak to Jesus, if I could, please."

The president? She nearly scoffed. What kind of fool did these pranksters think she was? But . . . well, the voice *did* sound familiar, like the one she heard almost every night on the news. Could it be?

"Mrs. MacDonald? Are you still there?"

The phone almost fell out of her hand. She turned to Joe and said, "It's the president of the United States."

"I'll get Jesus."

Funny thing: Joe didn't much like the president. He didn't much like many liberals, and this one was so far to the left, he thought Bernie Sanders might look that way and be surprised to find someone all the way down there. This president had messed up a lot over the years. Everyone should have gone with the other candidate. Still, he'd harbored a fantasy of telling the leader of the free world off, and now that he had her on the phone, he had no desire to do so. Instead he went up to Jesus' room and told him about the call.

"Thanks, Joe." And he started downstairs. No fanfare at all. Joe could have just told him that dinner was ready, and he would have gotten the same response.

Jesus spoke to the president for maybe two minutes, and then he hung up. "She's sending Air Force One for us. We should be at the airport by noon."

"Us? You mean, I'm going to meet the president?"

"I need you, Joe. Remember what I said."

"I . . . I didn't vote for her, though."

Jesus laughed, clapping Joe on the shoulder. "I don't think she'll care about that. Not today, at least."

Joe looked at Ursula, wondering if he should leave her so soon after just coming back.

She smiled. "You go, Joe. I know this is important to you. Besides, Rich has been a godsend around here."

Joe gave her the money from yesterday. "I think you should buy a new car with this. But buy whatever you think we might need, okay?"

"Joe! Where did you get this money?"

"It's—"

"We can't take this! You return this right away!"

"Don't worry about it, Ursula," Jesus said. "I gave it to him. I also want to give you some advice: spend it quickly. Soon it won't be worth anything."

"But . . . what?"

"I'll explain it later," Joe said. "Get Rich to take you to a car dealership. A good place. All right?"

Ursula nodded. "Okay, Joe. You know what's best."

He patted her hand, offering her a smile.

They packed again, and before long they drove out to meet with the president's own private jet.

This was only the third flight of Joe's life, and he couldn't get used to the absolute horror or being flung into the sky in such a fashion. But he found a great deal of enjoyment in the opulence of the amenities provided by the president. He found a library of the president's favorite movies and smiled when he saw the nation's leader loved Chuck Norris flicks. He didn't expect that from a woman.

Can't get more American than that. Too bad she's a liberal.

A half-hour after they touched down in Washington, DC, they arrived at the White House and were ushered in safely past the crowd that flooded 1600 Pennsylvania Avenue. After wending their way through hidden corridors, their guide brought them to the Oval Office.

Joe felt something crowd up in his throat, and he felt like crying for some reason. He couldn't understand why, but suddenly it felt like his heart was too big for his chest. Looking through the doorway he could see the President of the United States hunched over her desk, reading something on her iPad. She kept tapping the screen with a stylus, an annoyed look on her face.

She looked bigger than Joe had expected.

Dear Lord. I'm going to meet the president.

The thought scared the heck out of him.

The guide spoke with the president for a moment and then rushed back to the door. "She's ready for you. Please, follow me."

They entered, and the guide presented them. "Madam President, I'd like to introduce you to Jesus Christ and his aide, Joe MacDonald. Gentlemen, the President of the United States." He gestured across the desk.

The president regarded them both for a moment, but she paid closer attention to Jesus, trying to read him. Perhaps even working an angle. Absently, she put the iPad aside and leaned back in her chair. "I saw you on Fox. They're running that interview over and over again. Have a seat." She nodded to a set of couches and chairs in the center of the room.

After Jesus and Joe took one of the couches, the president took one of the chairs, crossing her legs. She cleared her throat, as if buying time. "Look. Is this for real? I mean, it looks real, but I can think of any number of stage magicians who could do this. I have to ask, are you really Jesus Christ?"

Jesus beamed. "I am."

"Well . . . I'm thinking of a number between one and a hundred. What is it?"

Joe stared at her, aghast. What kind of stupid question was that? Jesus wasn't a mind-reader. At least, he didn't think so. Why resort to a useless parlor trick?

"Forty-nine," Jesus said.

An eyebrow arched on the president's forehead. "Okay, you're right. But I guess that wasn't too special. Let's try something else." She produced a glass of water.

"Wine?" Jesus asked.

The president looked a bit nervous for a second, like she didn't want to say what she had on her mind. She fidgeted a moment. Then: "Do you do whiskey?"

Jesus waved his hand, and the water darkened to a rich amber right away. "I do beer, rum, scotch, heck. You name the alcoholic beverage, I do it."

The president sniffed at the glass, and both eyes widened. "How did you do that?"

Jesus answered with a shrug. Nothing more.

The president took a demure sip and set the glass aside. "I think I'm going to need a good drink for this conversation."

"I know it's difficult to accept," Jesus said, "but I'm here to change the world. I think I'm making some pretty good progress."

"Ah! I got it. Here." The president rolled up her pants leg to the knee, and she pointed to a nasty stretch of scar tissue. "I got this when I was a kid. Fell off a bike and down a gravelly hill. If you can fix this, I think we can do business."

"Sure thing."

Joe turned his head. He thought about warning the president about it, but he didn't think she would listen. She would have to learn for herself, like everyone else.

A flash. A gasp. An incredulous, "Wow."

Joe turned and saw the president's knee looked fresh. No scar.

She let the pants leg drop before she got to her knees, just like everyone else, and prayed for forgiveness. Honestly, the whole thing started to bore Joe. He'd seen it too many times—heck, he'd lived it once—and the novelty now wore thin. Except . . . he got a little bit of pleasure out of seeing the president like that. Liberals thought they knew everything.

Shame flushed through Joe's guts. He knew he shouldn't think like that, especially now that Jesus was here to save the world, but he couldn't help it. Some rivalries died hard.

He tried to find love in his heart for the president and found nothing. It would be something he'd have to work on.

"Now that *that's* out of the way," Jesus said. "Let's get down to business. We've got a lot to talk about."

"Of course." Jesus had already pulled the president off his knees, so now she settled comfortably back into her chair. "What did you have in mind?"

"We need to make a lot of changes. The way things are in this country, it's not very conducive to my message of love. The world isn't that great at it, either, but America is in a position where if this country changes for the better, the majority of the rest of the world will follow. After that it will be a lot easier to find the doubters and change their minds on a personal level."

Joe watched them talk back and forth for about an hour, and he thought he managed to follow most of it. But, when Jesus mentioned changing the monetary system, it threw Joe for a loop. All he remembered from the Bible was something about rendering unto Caesar that which is Caesar's, and that's as far as money went in the Good Book.

Jesus wanted to get rid of the very concept of money. He wanted the United States to return to a barter system. This would eliminate the classes, and without that barrier it would make love easier to achieve.

"Ooh, that's not going to fly with the rest of the world," the president said. "You *do* realize how much everyone else depends on our financial aid . . . ?"

"They'll fall in line. Things might even get better when they realize they no longer owe you money."

The president offered a skeptical laugh. "I'll believe it when I see it."

So that's what Jesus meant about money not being worth anything soon. Joe felt greed flush through his system as he hoped Ursula would spend it as quickly as possible. The president seemed to think these changes weren't very likely to be effective, but Joe had seen how quickly Jesus moved. By the end of the week, if they still had cash, they might as well burn it.

The conversation continued, and even though the president threw in a snarky comment every now and then, they shook hands at the conclusion, agreeing to get the ball rolling. The president even shook Joe's hand, thanking him for bringing Jesus.

"He brought me," Joe said.

The press already knew about this meeting, and thousands of reporters flooded the area around the White House. The president made a call and arranged for a few of them to be let into the Rose Garden for a quick conference. Before long the trio faced a collection of hopeful, eager faces.

Joe stepped back from the president and Jesus. He felt kind of tempted to be a part of their presentation, but he knew that no one was here to see him. He stood at a respectful distance, wondering how the rest of the world would take this.

The president stared at the camera, waiting. The teleprompter wasn't on, which must have been very strange for her. Joe didn't think she ever gave a speech without someone else putting words into her mouth. When did that become normal? Why do presidents need speechwriters? Isn't it important for someone in such a high office to be able to communicate on their own?

Someone gave the president a countdown, but the two and one were silent. The guy pointed to the president, and a red light appeared on the camera.

"My fellow Americans," she said. "Today is

a day unlike any other. After a long period of confusion and doubt, we finally have answers as to the nature of our existence. Many of you have seen him on Fox News, and some of you have even been personally touched and healed by him. Behind me, to my right, is the son of God, Jesus Christ himself."

A little more than a half-mile away from the White House, Jamal al-Hazred waited under a tarp designed to blend in with the rest of the rooftop. He'd set it up early in the morning, before the sun had the chance to rise. He'd spent the hours since waiting, listening to the radio on low, anxious for this very moment. As soon as he'd learned that Jesus had arrived at the White House, Jamal pieced together the rocket launcher he'd smuggled past security over the course of the last day. Now, sitting in the shade from the shed that contained the roof access door, he peered through a pair of binoculars into the Rose Garden.

He'd never done anything like this. His older brothers had all been highly-regarded warriors in Allah's name. All three of them were probably enjoying their seventy-two virgins, and he wondered what that would be like.

Jamal was only sixteen years old, and he hadn't so much as seen a naked woman.

He'd been trained by the best, though, and he had faith in his ability to get this done. He'd better get it done. He'd heard stories about people who failed their missions, about what happened to their families.

But no, he wasn't here out of fear. He was here for honor.

He was at the very outside of the rocket launcher's range, but he knew he could hit his target. How many times had he done it back home?

The voice on the radio announced that the president was about to make a speech about the Infidel Jesus. Jamal touched the rocket launcher. When the moment came upon him, he would be uncovered for about five seconds before pulling the trigger. He knew the Great Satan's eyes were everywhere, on this day above all others. The chances were against them nailing him before he could nail Jesus and the president, but just in case, he wore a suicide vest. It wouldn't get many people—and it certainly wouldn't get the *right* people—but at least he'd be able to take a few infidels with him. The bomb could take the top three floors of this building with him, after all. That's where the most important businessmen liked to work.

There! In the binoculars he saw the president make her appearance with Jesus and some other guy. Jamal tracked them as they made their way to the lectern facing the reporters. Jamal waited for the president to address the press before he took up his rocket launcher. Blood bludgeoned his veins as his shaky hands guided the weapon to his shoulder so he could see through the sight.

The president made a gesture toward Jesus, who stepped toward the lectern. The press clapped.

The perfect moment.

Jamal stepped from cover and screamed his death cry to Allah. As soon as he had a bead on Jesus he fired, blowing out both of his eardrums as smoke shot from the back of the launcher. The sudden violence frazzled him so badly that he didn't even see the rocket emerge on its swift journey to send the so-called son of God to his death.

As Jesus approached the lectern, he felt an odd tickling at the back of his skull. Every time someone had tried causing him harm, he'd felt that strange sensation. Quickly he scanned the minds of the reporters, expecting an assassin with a gun.

The sweep of his telepathy reached pretty far, and he caught a few of Jamal's thoughts just in time to see, maybe a half-mile away, a screaming lunatic with a huge weapon. Jesus hadn't seen anything like it before, but as soon as he saw the rocket making its rapid approach, he knew it couldn't be good.

The Secret Service guys jumped into action, but anyone with half a brain knew it would be futile. Even if they managed to cover up their leader with their own bodies, it would do no good. The president was well and truly fucked.

Or she would be, if she didn't have Jesus on her side.

Jesus whipped his hand up, and even though the rocket still had maybe an eighth of a mile to go, it moved aside, as if it had been slapped. It advanced vertically into the sky until it exploded seconds later, harmlessly spewing smoke into the atmosphere. A few pieces of shrapnel pattered to the ground below, but touched no one. Jesus made sure of that.

The Secret Service ushered the president away, and one of them reached out to grab Jesus, too. "It's not safe, sir. We have to go."

"See to yourself," Jesus said. When the guy didn't desist, Jesus turned his most beatific smile on to him. "Dude, I'll be okay. Find some cover, all right?"

The Secret Service guy let his arm drop, and then his jaw dropped as he watched Jesus squat down and jump up. He flew into the sky like a superhero, blazing across the half-mile from the Rose Garden to the building where Jamal, clutching his bleeding ears, rolled around on the roof.

Jesus slammed down to the gravel surface, knees bent to allow for shock absorption, and he glared at the would-be assassin. "That was not cool, man."

Jamal, shocked, watched as Jesus moved toward him, quick as a mongoose. Panicked, Jamal grabbed for the detonator for his suicide vest. It never occurred to him that this would be the perfect way to end such a popular infidel; he just thought it would be the quickest way to escape Jesus' wrath.

Jesus flicked his fingers back, and the detonator zipped from Jamal's hand to his own. "If my brother had his way, I'd kick you off this building and push this button. You're a lucky man, Jamal al-Hazred."

He crushed the detonator in his hand as if

it had been a soda can and flung it aside. Grimacing, he grabbed the sides of Jamal's head and let his healing power flow through his fingers and into Jamal's brain.

Jamal screamed, blinded by the light and the hot sensation in his ears. Yet a moment later, when it was all done, he was surprised to learn he could hear again. "What . . . what did you do to me?"

"I healed you," Jesus said.

"But . . . why?"

"Because I love you, you big dummy."

Jamal couldn't believe his luck. He had another chance to eliminate Jesus. He never wondered how he'd been healed, and he didn't need to wonder. All he needed to do was kill Jesus for Allah.

"Don't bother, Jamal. Looks like my work isn't done yet."

He reached for the kid's chest, and Jamal leaped back, trying to escape. Jesus shot forward and touched Jamal where he needed to. Light poured into of him, and darkness seeped out of Jamal in a torrent of hatred.

When Jesus pulled back, Jamal collapsed to his knees, weeping. Never before in his entire life had he felt free from the hatred that coursed through his body like blood. Only now that it was gone did he feel overwhelming shame at his actions. His mental state couldn't stand it. He broke, tears and snot caking his face. Incomprehensible words poured from his mouth.

Jesus pulled him to his feet, but Jamal wasn't strong enough to remain standing.

Chuckling, Jesus scooped Jamal up into his arms and flew him down, back to the Rose Garden. By now helicopters hovered around them, men poking out the sides with giant machine guns.

Gently, Jesus landed, and he set Jamal down. Jamal curled up into a ball and sobbed every emotion he'd bottled up for sixteen years into the grass that pillowed beneath his head.

Men with guns surrounded Jamal. One of them shouted, "That's the one! Get him!"

"Whoa," Jesus said. "Take it easy. He's just a kid."

The head of the security team snarled. "This *kid* just tried to assassinate the President of the United States. He's going to be buttfucked for breakfast every day for the rest of his life. Those guys at Gitmo will wear him like a condom."

"No, they won't. He's under my protection."

The reporters all seemed to make the same gasping sound at the same point. No one could believe that Jesus wanted to spare a murderous motherfucker like that. It just didn't stand to reason. How could he *not* want to punish a monster like that, regardless of age?

"He tried to kill you," one of them said.

"He didn't succeed. And now I've healed his hatred. He's never going to do anything like this ever again." He stooped by Jamal's side, hugging the youth. "I forgive you, Jamal al-Hazred."

"Thank you! Thank you, Lord!"

"Stand down, captain." The president had returned, and she stood by the lectern, watching the whole display unfold.

"But—"

"That's an order."

The captain backed off, holstering his weapon, and the world watched as the reign of Jesus Christ began.

CHAPTER 7:
THE CHANGE

After such a benevolent act, everyone wanted to hear what Jesus had to say. Things moved quickly after Jamal's healing and forgiveness. The president abdicated her office, giving leadership of the nation over to Jesus, who quickly set about dismantling the government.

The world reeled as he did this. No one could believe such a great nation as the United States would allow this to happen. Yet one after the other, they fell under Jesus' sway, and the world became a safer, freer place one small piece at a time. In a world filled with love, no one needed soldiers. In a world free of greed, no one needed money. In a world of respect, no one discriminated against anyone.

Thus began a new age of wonder and love and celebration. There were holdouts, of course. The Vatican, for example, didn't want to cave in to the demands of the so-called savior. Jesus wanted them to dismantle the church and give up all their worldly possessions. Holy men could no longer live as rich men, and that stuck in their craw a bit.

Jesus had to visit the Pope and perform a few miracles before they got the idea, and soon the Vatican was no more.

By the end of the month, there were only a few holdouts. Israel turned their back on America, and Islam managed to keep up their own faith, even as the Hindus and Buddhists gave in. All in all, not bad for a month's work.

But one thing kept nagging at Jesus. He kept thinking back to Jamal, and how even someone like that could be turned, which spoke well for the few who still didn't believe in him. Yet . . . even Jesus knew he wasn't the *real* Jesus. He hadn't gone native. Generally speaking, human beings were insane. Sometimes they were capable of amazing acts of kindness. They were also capable of atrocities that would shock even some of the people back on Jesus' home planet, and Jesus came from a society of warriors.

Despite the wide range of human capacity, they were also incredibly gullible. How could a gathering of societies be driven by unreasoning stupidity? Jesus' world didn't have gods. They just had knowledge. Period. He couldn't get his head around why people would make shit up and then let it dictate their lives.

A portion of this certainly came from a group of slightly smarter people wanting to rule over the minds of the rest, of course, but to let it become such a trenchant part of their societies that an atheist would not be welcome anywhere on earth? A nonbeliever could have never become president of the United States, for example.

It made conquering this planet so easy, but it also bothered Jesus a bit. War dominated his own world, and he'd been raised by the strongest family organization in history. His father ruled the entire galaxy, which only got bigger as Jesus' brothers spread throughout the universe and conquered more planets.

Back home, Jesus had been an oddball. He could do all the things his brothers excelled at, which ran the gamut from strategy to cold-blooded murder, but unlike his siblings he didn't *like* it. He'd seen them joking as they slaughtered entire world populations. They played games with corpses. They took great pleasure in murdering children in front of their parents. They recorded their most horrible acts and played them back at parties as a greatest hits compilation for which they were greatly rewarded by their father.

Jesus never did that. No, he committed those acts alongside his brothers, but he never got off on it. He always knew there had to be an better way to conquer planets. Bloodless ways. Ways that would end with both sides being genial to each other. Not everything should be achieved through annihilation.

What good was possessing the universe if everyone in it feared you? What would get done? Too much time would be spent quelling rebellions.

Jesus, who kind of liked being called Jesus

rather than his actual name, found himself liking human beings despite their wacky beliefs.

CHAPTER 8: LOVERS

Jesus could have lived anywhere in the world. Most wanted him to live in the White House, and others thought he should take up residence in the Middle East, where this whole thing began. Whenever he traveled, he stayed with whoever offered to put him up for the night. But, in America, he did his very best to stay with Joe MacDonald and his family.

They'd made good use of the money he'd given them before money became worthless. They had a new car and had been able to repair their house and farm fairly well. But, for the most part, the farm remained the same, and Jesus liked the simplicity of it. He liked the silence of the middle of nowhere.

Joe had taken to dressing a bit nicer, but he still acted the same as ever. Always pleased to have Jesus under his roof, he never could get over his own star-struck nature. Even after all this time he couldn't believe he was one of Jesus' closest friends, if not *the* closest.

By this time, Jesus had gotten a haircut and had shaved his beard down close to his cheeks. He also started dressing in a t-shirt and jeans. It had taken people a while to get used to seeing him like that, but he felt much more comfortable this way. Not only that, but it seemed to eliminate a mysterious force around him. When he'd dressed up for the shows people always felt a bit distant because he looked important and was on TV. Now that he'd loosened up, people found him to be more approachable. There were very few people left in the world that he hadn't healed yet, but those few very quickly rectified the matter by finding comfort in approaching him.

He liked that.

This night, as he finished up dinner with the MacDonalds, he felt more relaxed than he ever had since he'd arrived on earth. Things had been very busy, and for the first time in a while he'd done nothing but hang out. This had been a vacation day for him, since tomorrow he planned on traveling to the Middle East to talk with Muslim leadership. The president, who now acted as a consultant for Jesus, suggested bringing a military force, just in case.

"I'll be fine," Jesus said. "They can't kill me."

"It can't hurt."

"Sure it can. If I arrive with backup, they'll be suspicious of me. No, I'm going it alone. Thanks for the advice, though."

He leaned back in his chair, in Joe and Ursula's kitchen, grinning as he rubbed his belly. A belch rumbled in the back of his throat, and he politely held back, letting it rattle around behind his tongue.

"That was great, Ursula. One of the finest meals I've ever had."

"I'm glad you liked it," she said.

"I think I'm going to sit out on the porch for a while. Get some fresh night air before I have to hit the road tomorrow. The air always tastes the best out here."

"It tastes much better elsewhere, too," Joe said. "I'm still surprised that you managed to disband the oil companies. I didn't think anyone could do it."

"It was a necessary step. This planet is too important to be riddled with pollution. Besides, those guys were pretty corrupt. They needed a wakeup call, and I think they got it."

"You did more good than you can ever imagine with that one, Jesus," Joe said. "You want company?"

"Sure. Come on."

Once outside, they both sat in chairs facing out into the growing dusk, and the smell of corn wafted back to them. Ordinarily, Joe would light his pipe on a night like this, but now he didn't care for tobacco. He wondered if maybe Jesus had cured him of his addiction. Now he found contentment in just sitting and looking out at his property, taking in the whirring of the crickets and the fecund smell of the earth.

"We've come a long way in such a small amount of time," Joe said.

"My main job is almost over," Jesus said. "The most important part is to get everyone in the world onboard. After that, there will be a bigger job for us all. It's going to take a lot of strength and vigor. Do you think everyone's up to it?"

Joe flexed his muscles, grinning. "I'm stronger than I've ever been, and something tells me the same thing holds true of the rest of the world, or at least everyone you've cured."

"I hope so. It'll be a lot harder than accepting me into their hearts. I'm talking physical labor, here."

"I'm used to it, but a lot of people have been used to desk jobs in this country. They might be a bit soft, but they'll probably step up. Everyone loves you, Jesus. You know that. They would all die for you, me included."

Jesus patted Joe's shoulder. "Thanks, man. I appreciate hearing it. But I hope it doesn't come to anyone dying for me. I think there have been enough people dying in my name over the centuries. Even worse, *killing* in my name. I'm still baffled by that one."

Joe opened his mouth to say something, but he seemed suddenly distracted. Jesus sent out his mental feelers and sensed a slight crackle in the air, just like the feeling whenever he was about to receive a message from home. He'd forgotten about the month he'd been given. He suddenly found himself wishing his home planet had forgotten, too.

Except -- something about this one felt different. Hotter. He could almost feel the burning in the back of his mind.

"You feel it, too?" Joe asked.

Before Jesus could answer, the air sizzled, and something rocketed over Joe's house. It whistled loud enough to rock the windows in their panes, and it left a smell like burning ozone as it trailed across the sky. Then, it vanished into the crops and landed with a loud thump. It shook the ground, and they could feel its vibration through their chests as if their stomachs had rumbled with hunger.

Both of them stood up, awed.

"What the heck was that?" Joe asked.

"I . . . I don't know." Although he had a pretty good idea.

"It's just like when you showed up. Freaky."

Jesus glanced over to him. "Stay here. Inside, with your family. I'm going to check it out. I'll be back."

"You sure you don't want help?"

"Just wait here, okay?"

Joe nodded, retreating toward the door. He watched as Jesus hopped off the porch and took to the sky, soaring like a superhero. He'd seen Jesus do this once before, at the Rose Garden, but he couldn't get used to it. How could someone fly like that, even someone like Jesus? He couldn't even do that in the Bible. Well, probably not, at any rate.

Jesus rarely flew on this planet, and at first he felt his stomach shift around inside of him. It took him a moment to get used to it again as he ripped across the cornfield, seeking out the object that had just landed. He scanned the horizon, looking for the telltale smoke and fire.

There! He hovered for a moment, orbiting

the scorched hole in the middle of the cornfield. It took him a moment to realize that this was the same spot he'd come down when he first arrived. Such utter precision only meant one thing.

A hand emerged from the crater, and it clutched at the dirt, pulling. Soon, a body followed. It was a disguise, just like Jesus' own, but he could recognize the being under the façade.

Jesus floated to the ground and confronted the newcomer, whose body—completely naked—was a rich tan color. A huge beard with a very pointy mustache covered most of his face. It took him a moment to get it, and when he did he couldn't help but laugh.

"What's so funny?"

"I wouldn't have expected you to show up as Muhammad," Jesus said. "What, did you look at one of their books on gods and point at a random page? You do realize that our followers hate each other, right?"

"I didn't think much about it. But fuck that shit. Do you know why I'm here?"

"The month is up."

"And do you have a progress report? Or have you been neglecting those for a reason?"

Jesus touched both of Muhammad's shoulders, rubbing them up and down. "Can't all that wait? It's been a while since I've seen someone from home, much less you."

"You know that—"

Jesus silenced Muhammad by drawing him close and laying a gentle kiss on his lips. They looked into each others eyes for a moment, and Muhammad softened up. He reached both hands behind Jesus' head, twining his fingers in his hair, and this time their kiss was deeper, more passionate. Their tongues wrestled against each other, and when they pulled back, saliva wetly shone like diamonds in their beards.

"Not here," Jesus said. "Someone might see."

"Who cares? Fuck these people. They're slaves. They're—"

"Not to me. I have to keep up the charade."

"If they see, we'll just kill them."

Jesus shook his head. "That's not how I'm doing this."

Muhammad sighed. "Fine. Where, then?"

Jesus pointed up. "To the moon, Muhammad." And he grabbed his lover's hand.

In unison they both soared into the sky. As they drew closer to the stratosphere they each took a deep breath—enough to last them for a while—and before long they found themselves breaking through the clouds and into space. Still propelled by the force of their power, they floated toward the moon, and in no time they gently came to rest on its surface.

They locked eyes, and Jesus sent his lover this thought: *Do you think Muhammad had a cock that big?*

And you didn't give yourself a huge piece? Muhammad asked. Then he fell to his knees and worked at the front of Jesus' pants. A moment later Jesus' hard, throbbing dick stuck out, pointing just over Muhammad's shoulder.

Muhammad didn't wait for anything. He pulled his tongue back so it would cover the way to his lungs, and he opened his mouth, plugging it with Jesus' member.

It's been so long. Jesus moaned. He felt himself drawn in, and his balls slipped around opposite sides of Muhammad's chin. For all of this time, he'd robbed himself of pleasure like this. He felt it wouldn't have sold the right image to the humans. Now he felt ready to shoot off already.

Don't you dare. Not yet.

Jesus smiled, pulling himself from Muhammad's mouth. He drew his lover up, and they stood facing each other, their dicks side by side. *I think I might have an inch up on you.*

Fuck you.

In a second. Jesus wrapped his hands around both of their cocks, stroking them together. It felt like they'd become one flesh in that moment, experiencing each others pleasure.

Enough play, Muhammad said. *I want you to fuck the shit out of me.*

Jesus twisted Muhammad's body, forcing him around, and pushed him to his knees, bending him at the waist. The sunlight from around the earth lit up Muhammad's ass perfectly, and Jesus could see the all-familiar pucker at the back. His hard-on, still slick from Muhammad's spit, almost glowed as he stooped down behind his lover and touched his glans to the open, inviting butthole. The two fit together like they were made for each other, like adjacent puzzle pieces.

Put it in me.

Jesus grabbed Muhammad's hips and pulled back, impaling him on a heavy, precum-dripping cock. Pleasure oozed throughout his entire body as he picked up the pace, thrusting in and out of Muhammad's ass as Muhammad pushed back hard. Jesus felt like he could touch Muhammad's guts as he plowed on and on.

Muhammad tried to pull back, eager for his turn, but Jesus pushed him down, wrapping his arms around Muhammad's waist for maximum penetration. Mentally growling, Jesus bit Muhammad on the neck, working his head back and forth as if he wanted to tear a hunk out.

Oh! Muhammad gasped. *Do that again!*

Jesus did, and Muhammad squirmed. Then, for the first time in ages, Jesus shot his load, filling Muhammad with at least a half-year's worth of cum. Then, mentally panting, he pulled back and let his flaccid penis slip out, covered in semen and shit. It steamed in the freezing cold of the moon.

Muhammad snarled, pouncing on Jesus, savagely turning him over and spreading his ass cheeks. *You ready for some of this?*

I've been waiting for so long. Do it.

Muhammad rubbed his dick in the mess that had oozed out of him, getting it nice and slick, and then holding a thumb against the glans, he sheathed it in Jesus' asshole. Deep.

Jesus nearly let out a yelp, but he managed to contain himself as Muhammad began to work.

His lover hadn't spent so long on earth, and as a result he could last longer. It took Muhammad nearly forty-five minutes of thrusting and twisting to get off. Unlike Jesus, though, he pulled out and ejaculated, aiming for Jesus' back.

The lack of gravity didn't allow for it. Gobs of cum floated above Muhammad's ripe cock. It would eventually come back down, but Muhammad didn't have the patience for it. He grabbed Jesus' hips and pulled up, making sure to strike the cum with his lover. Finally it spread out across his flesh, and Muhammad's dick stopped spouting.

Only then did they come apart. Jesus and Muhammad kissed for just a moment, and then Jesus started getting dressed. As he did so, Muhammad cast a glance behind him. They'd been fucking very close to a stiff, spread out American flag. He saw a few footprints nearby that belonged to neither him nor Jesus.

What's this shit?

Jesus finished buckling his belt and looked over to Muhammad. *Humans were here. Didn't you know that?*

They knew how to get off their miserable planet? That's unusual. Usually these lowlifes are too stupid or superstitious for that kind of thing.

Jesus nodded over to a plaque. *They left a message. See?*

Muhammad ignored it. Instead he swept his own foot over the leavings of the astronauts, leveling them out before replacing them with his own prints.

Stop that! You're ruining a piece of history.

Who gives a fuck? In a hundred years, these humans won't even exist. I don't want to leave a trace of them behind.

What have I told you? You've got to do things my way. I'm almost there. I can taste it. We're almost ready.

Muhammad glared at him. *I can't believe you're still going on about this. It's been a month, and you still don't have them ready for the next phase. You do realize we're running out of supplies, right?*

Yes. Yes, you bastard. I'm aware of it. And we'll have some soon. I just have a few more humans to manipulate, and then we can get to work. By this time next month—

No. No more promises. You've got to show results. You should have just enslaved these people like we told you to. Your time is up.

Jesus shook his head. He didn't say another word. What else could he say?

You're an obstinate little shit, you know that? If Father were here to see you like this, he'd shit a new son out.

Jesus stared his lover, his brother, dead in the eyes, but still he said nothing.

Have it your way, Xa—

No. That's not my name, so don't say it. For now.

Have you gone native?!

121

Jesus didn't answer.

This is it. I'm going home, and I'm going to come back with a group of warriors. If you don't have those supplies, we're going to level the planet and take it for ourselves. Do you understand?

Jesus blanched. Muhammad really wouldn't do that, would he?

Muhammad plucked the American flag from the ground like a flower, and he wiped his messy cock and asshole off with it. Then he snapped the staff it had been attached to and flung it away. It would be a while before it came back down to rest on the moon.

This is your last chance. Don't fuck it up.

Muhammad shot himself off the surface of the moon, hurtling towards deep space. Jesus watched after him until he became a speck of nothing in the distance. He sighed.

Now, he looked back at the earth, and he wondered if maybe Muhammad had been right. Maybe human beings needed to be treated like animals instead of intelligent creatures. Maybe it would be better to end the charade and get down to the dirty business he was really here for.

Just then, he looked away from the planet, ashamed. His eyes found the plaque the astronauts had left behind, and he casually read it. "Here men from the planet Earth first set foot upon the Moon, July 1969 A.D. We came in peace for all mankind."

His vision blurred, and tears froze on his face. These human beings weren't just capable of wondrous things. They were also amazing poets. To blast themselves away from the safety of their home world, and to come all this way just to write one of the most beautiful things he'd ever read.

No. Muhammad was wrong. These humans could get up to all sorts of horrible shit, but they were sentient beings. They had every right to live free, and he would protect that, even if it meant turning his back on his own people.

Angry and aflame with righteousness, he jumped from the moon and soared through space between it and the earth. His clothes burned away as he reentered the planet's atmosphere, but he remained unscathed. Last time he'd come from another galaxy, but this time it was only a hop, skip and jump away, so he didn't come down hard enough to cause a crater.. He landed gently and finally let out his breath, taking another in.

He took in the scent around him, not just of the earth but of its people, and he felt strong enough to take on an entire race of warriors if it came to that.

It probably would.

Back at the house Joe waited for him on the porch, a shotgun in his hand. The rusty old thing probably wouldn't fire, but Jesus knew a lot of humans felt safer with a gun in their hands, even if said gun wouldn't be able to do much good.

"You okay?" Joe asked.

"I'm fine. You can put that away."

Joe set the shotgun down and propped it up against one of the beams on the porch.

"What was it?"

Jesus considered telling his friend that it was trouble. He wouldn't have spelled that trouble out, but it would be better to be on guard, wouldn't it? Jesus decided to not tell him. When Muhammad came back with an army, this world would suffer a great deal. Why not let him enjoy the calm before the storm?

"A meteor," Jesus said. "Nothing more."

Joe trusted Jesus so much, he didn't question the answer. Jesus felt a pang of guilt about that. Even though humans were incredibly gullible, it didn't make him feel any better about tricking them. He wondered what they would do if he told them the truth about everything. He could never do that, though. They'd never do what he needed them to do if he did. Muhammad would then have no choice but to beat them into submission.

"Let's go inside," Jesus said. "It's getting late."

The kids had already been tucked in, and Joe and Ursula took their leave of Jesus for the night. He spent most of the night sitting in the living room and drinking whiskey he made from the well water out back.

He liked the sounds of the night in the middle of nowhere. No cars rushed by. Only the crickets outside, and the slow creaking of the house as it settled registered in his ears. It was very relaxing.

Taking on his brother and the rest of his family would be next to impossible. If he tried to directly engage them, he would lose the planet to them quickly. He had to move up his timetable. If he didn't have something to show for his time here, the human race would be fucked.

Could it be that he'd enjoyed playing a messiah so much that he lost the plot?

Maybe, if he pushed himself, he could have enough to sate Muhammad's need. He'd probably have to get started tomorrow.

So much for taking some time off.

He stood to go to bed, but he had whiskey legs. Before he stumbled he turned the whiskey in his blood back to water, and he sobered up immediately. On his way up to bed he paused outside the boys' room and listened to them snoring softly. In the next room over he could hear Joe and Ursula trying to be quiet as they made love.

This felt like a real family. Back home Jesus had never known one, not like this. For the first time in his life he felt like he belonged somewhere. Earth was worth fighting for. It was his last thought just as he went to bed, and it was his first thought upon awakening the next day.

He might not have been Jesus Christ, but he had a lot of special powers, enough so that everyone believed in him. Maybe it was time to be a messiah for real.

CHAPTER 9:
THE SERMON ON THE
MOUNT

Within a week, the final pockets of Islam gave in and accepted Jesus Christ as their lord and savior. It took a little more deception on Jesus' part than usual to get this done. He thought about Jamal al-Hazred a lot, and he figured that if he let something like that happen again, on a much bigger scale, then he would be able to turn the tide.

He visited the Middle East openly and without shelter. It would only be a matter of time before they struck at him. He just had to be sure to have media around him at all times, so as to catch the assassination attempt on live television.

They tried to get him with rocket launchers and bullets, and he managed to deflect them all. When this failed they threw suicide bombers at him, but he read their minds and was able to disarm them before they could hurt anyone, including themselves. In the process, though, one of the suicide bombers accidentally set his charge off early, and he blew himself in two.

Luckily for him, he still lived. Jesus could heal anything, even explosive damage like this, but resurrection was beyond his abilities. When he saved the suicide bomber's life in front of the world—healing his wounds without leaving so much as a scar—Islam gave up the fight and joined everyone else under Jesus' sway.

Israel fell in line the next day after, when they tried something similar and failed. Finally, after months of struggle, the world belonged to Jesus. He'd finally succeeded where even his own people swore he would fail.

All that remained was one final thing: to get humanity to do what he came here to get them to do. For that, he figured, there should be a bit of symbolism involved. Humans loved that kind of thing, and if he was being honest with himself, it pleasantly tickled some core part of his brain, too.

Too bad there were no mountains in Galilee. In fact, it would seem that no one knew for sure where the original Sermon on the Mount had taken place. Jesus had done his research, though, and he knew the most likely suspect was a place called the Mount of the Beatitudes.

The day after Israel surrendered to his will, he went to the Mount, accompanied by Joe and a camera crew, as well as a swarm of followers eager for the new word of the Christ.

Once Jesus got there, he felt kind of

disappointed. He was hoping for something a bit more dramatic, but the mountain was more of a hill. Standing above the crowd didn't feel as awesome as he'd expected when he first started thinking about this moment, before he had even come to earth. Still, it would have to do.

The cameras were readied, and the crew helped Jesus test the microphone, which was also hooked up to an amazing sound system that would probably broadcast his words throughout the rest of the country.

Just for the hell of it, Jesus fed the masses with five loaves and two fish. It seemed to get a laugh out of those who got it, but even more importantly, it helped put him into a symbolic frame of mind.

He took a deep breath and reminded himself that this was the performance he'd been waiting to give for so many years. This had been part of his scheme even before anything else had come to mind.

The cameraman gave him a thumbs-up, and Jesus cleared his throat. The sound rumbled through the hills of Galilee, and everyone cheered.

"Two thousand years ago," he said, "I stood right here and delivered the first Sermon on the Mount. I have returned to you today for another sermon, but it is not one you would expect from me."

The crowd silenced itself, waiting eagerly for new words of wisdom from the Messiah.

"Yesterday a door closed on a terrible era of human history. Unprecedented hatred has lived in the veins of humanity for so long, no one even notices it anymore. Hatred for people who look different from you. Hatred for people who don't share the same sexual proclivities as you. Hatred for people who have different sex organs than you. Hatred for those who don't share your financial status. I'm glad to say it's all over. Yesterday the last vestiges of this world who lived with hatred in their hearts gave in. They surrendered to the love of their fellow human beings. From here on out everything is changed."

Cheers. Jesus let them go on for a moment, but then he held up his hands. Everyone grew quiet again.

"Last time I was here I preached that we needed to give up the Old Testament ways. We needed to practice love instead of violence. No one wanted to buy it back then, and if I hadn't come back to remove doubt from the doubters, I don't think you'd buy it this time, either. But, I *did* remove doubt. The very fact that Israelis and Palestinians stand shoulder to shoulder in brotherly love in this very crowd is proof of this. Protestants and Catholics are now embracing each other in Ireland. The KKK and the Nation of Islam in America are now breaking bread together. All of this is possible because there is so much love in this world.

"But, I do want to remind you that the old ways need to stay gone forever. For too long humanity has suffered from deranged mental illness, and now that we're free of it, we can't backslide into old practices. I may not always be here to remind you."

"Who would dare crucify you today?" someone in the crowd shouted.

Jesus smiled, hoping he appeared as enigmatic as he thought. "There will soon come a day when I leave you to travel to other worlds. You are not God's only creation in the universe."

Gasps and other sounds of awe came back to him. Perfect. Time to bring them to the point.

"In a world of absolute love, the days of hatred are over. In a world where there is no money, the days of greed are over. In a world where everyone owns everything, the days of war are over. This is the dawn of a new era, one where people don't do good works out of some egotistical need to be noticed. From here on, everyone will do good works because they want to. Last time I condemned people for doing the former. Now, they simply can't. The choice is out of their hands.

"The days of judgment are over. No one can judge anyone else, and there are no false prophets to fear."

Again, more cheers. Jesus let this one go on for a while longer than before. When it died out naturally, he continued:

"What is there to do, now that the human race has been saved? There is still a lot of work to be done. Luckily, I've healed you all and given you all strong backs, because you will need them. The planet is not out of danger, not yet.

"The resources you have used to power the earth are the very things that will eventually cause its destruction. That's why we're going to need to work together to harvest as much oil and natural gas as possible. Coal and uranium have to go, as well. If we don't get rid of these things, the planet is going to self-destruct."

Jesus paused, waiting for someone to interrupt him. Even to his own ears, he sounded false. Surely someone among the humans would recognize his lie.

Then again, they *were* pretty gullible. No one voiced dissention. Time to push them a little further.

"We're also going to need to strip the planet of iron, copper, silver and gold. We're going to have to do it as soon as possible. We can load all of these things together, and I'll fly them out to a safe spot in space. My father has sent a group of angels our way, and they're going to help rid this planet of these dangerous things."

Again he paused, and yet again no one expressed disbelief.

"This is going to be a worldwide initiative, and I'm putting my right hand man in charge of this effort. You all know Joe MacDonald by now." He gestured to Joe, who stared back at him, flabbergasted. The crowd cheered. "Do whatever he says. He speaks on my behalf in my absence."

The applause reached its crescendo, and Jesus felt waves of love and adulation running through him, making his heart soar.

Finally the sound died down, and Jesus hit the home stretch. "I used to talk about who are blessed and why they're blessed. The days of beatitudes are over, as well. Blessed are all of us, who are all things at all times. You don't have to wait until death for your reward. You have it here and now, on this wonderful planet, the third from the sun. Thank you for listening, everyone. And I love you, one and all."

He closed his eyes and knelt before the crowd as they shouted their love for him back. He smiled, pleased that the whole thing had gone off without a hitch.

But, he certainly didn't feel happy. He felt bad for the way he'd played them. Still, in the end their lives would possibly be saved because he lied to them today. That had to be worth something, right?

Later that night Jesus and Joe retired to their room at the Diaghilev in Tel Aviv. Joe waited until he heard their people shuffle away, leaving only the guards outside. Jesus had told everyone time and again that he didn't need to be protected, but it seemed to make the humans feel better about themselves, so he allowed the detail.

Joe said, "Can I talk to you for a second?"

"You can talk to me whenever you want," Jesus said. He unbuttoned his shirt and started shrugging out of it. "But I'd appreciate it if you'd hurry. I could sure use a shower."

Joe didn't even waste time promising to be quick. He launched right into it. "Why did you put me in charge of this project? I have no experience with this kind of thing. I don't know the first thing about doing, well, whatever the heck you want me to do. I don't understand it."

"You don't think you can do it?"

Joe stared at him for a moment, his mouth working. After a couple of false starts, he decided to go with the swift truth. "Frankly, no."

"You don't think much of yourself, then. I've known you for a few months, and I'm certain you can do it. I don't give people tasks if I don't think they can succeed."

"I'm just a farmer. Can I manage everything *that* involves? Sure. I'm basically the boss of my own company, where I do most of the work. I have no problem with that. But *this*? This is too big."

Jesus kicked out of his trousers and wrapped a towel around his waist. He turned to face his friend. "This is essentially the same job. Instead of farming crops, you're removing unhealthy and dangerous things from the dirt. And you'll have a lot of people at your beck and call. Yes, it's big, but it's only a bigger version of what you've done your whole life."

"I don't know . . ."

Jesus touched Joe's cheek. "I have faith in you."

Elation bloomed in Joe's heart, and he couldn't help but return Jesus' omnipresent smile. "Thank you."

As dusk became dark Jesus emerged from the shower and put on a robe, which he then wore into the main room. Joe sat at the bar, sipping cautiously at a drink he'd made from an airplane bottle in the mini-fridge.

"What are you doing?" Jesus asked.

"I've never been much of a drinker. I mean, I had my days when I was a teenager, tearing up the back roads of my hometown in my father's old Charger with my friends. We never did anything too crazy, but we had some fun. I'm glad those days are behind me now, of course. Even after you healed me, I don't think I could go back to that way of living."

Jesus took a peek into Joe's head. The vibes radiating from his friend were odd and out of place. He wanted to find out what had brought on this strange reminiscence.

"The sauce got my father," Joe said. "He was a decent man. I didn't think so at the time. Back then I thought he was a tyrant, but now that I'm the age he was when he died, now that I have kids of my own, I understand. I wish I could have told him that. Heck, I guess I'm not telling you anything you didn't already know."

Jesus nodded, still looking around. He suspected Joe didn't even know where he was going with this, either.

There! Suddenly Jesus understood it, just before Joe opened his mouth to continue. "That part about Lazarus. Can you really bring back the dead?"

"I can," Jesus said, "but my father doesn't want me to do that anymore. I acted on my own when it came to poor Lazarus. I brought him back, but that meant dragging him back out of Heaven into the Hell of a decomposing body. He spent the rest of his days feared and reviled. If you're asking me to do that again, I'm going to have to say no."

Joe took a sip from his drink and put the glass down on the bar, directly onto the sweat ring that had already been there. The ice jingled for a moment, and all went silent in the hotel room. "Are we going to die?" he asked.

Did Joe suspect something about his task? Did he even catch a glimpse of Muhammad? Jesus started shuffling through Joe's head again, but a moment later he realized he didn't need to.

"Now that you've healed us all," Joe said. "Are we immortal? Or will we live forever unless someone kills us?"

"Joe, I healed you, but you're not going to live forever. One day you'll die and go to Heaven. That's what my father wants, after all. None of this would be worth it without all humans dying and going to Heaven."

Joe sighed with relief and wiped at his eyes. "Thank God. I was afraid I'd never get to see my own father ever again."

Jesus hugged his friend close and felt Joe's grief, some of it as old as the death of his father, pour out of him. In that moment, as Jesus held him, he considered telling Joe the truth. Maybe it would make everything easier if everyone knew what was really happening. It would definitely ease Jesus' guilt and shame.

No. He was too far into the lie. He had to see this thing through and hope for the best.

Joe, who hadn't had anything stronger than the occasional beer, didn't handle the hard liquor he'd ingested well. Woozy, he started passing out in Jesus' arms. Jesus sensed this and walked Joe to his bed. Tucked him in. Kissed him on the forehead.

It would be a long time before Jesus got any sleep for himself.

CHAPTER 10:
PROGRESS AND REPRIEVE

Joe MacDonald worked quicker than anyone expected in his new role. The day after the Sermon, he attacked his job with great vigor, and before long he had crews all around the world working at ridding the earth of her poisons. All the while, those who were not versed in manual labor were put to work creating windmills and solar panels. A shocking amount of work got done that first week. At the end of each day, Jesus flew the fuel and rocks up to the moon, where he hoped to hand it all off to his brother before Muhammad could attack his adopted planet.

Joe couldn't make it back to visit his home very often, but he had someone teach him how to use Skype so he could get the next best thing. At the end of each conversation he would hold his hand up to his webcam, and his sons would reach back to him. For Ursula, he kissed the camera as she kissed hers.

Jesus knew it wouldn't be long before Muhammad returned with reinforcements, so he pressured Joe a little to get things moving faster. Material was piling up quickly on the moon—the dark side, so as to avoid attention should Muhammad return early—and soon, he thought he might have enough to satisfy his home world.

One week and a day from the moment Jesus finished the new Sermon on the Mount, he started sensing that all-too-familiar crackle in the air. It felt more intense than the other times. By Jesus' estimation, Muhammad was bringing a team of ten. He couldn't possibly take them all. The only way this would end without bloodshed would be if Muhammad accepted the resources he had.

Jesus took a deep breath and shot into the sky, and when he entered space he saw his brother waiting for him. Alone. Did he feel the need to hide the others? Surely he knew that Jesus could detect them.

Muhammad nodded toward the moon, and the two of them returned to the very spot they had made love. The marks of their passion were still etched in the dirt where once there had been astronaut footprints.

I'd be very careful if I were you, Muhammad sent to him. *I have ten more companions. I left them on Mars, but they can be here in thirteen minutes. I hope that won't be necessary.*

Jesus shook his head. *I have the planet under my sway. I also have presents for you to bring back home.*

Muhammad followed as Jesus led them across the surface of the moon, over to the dark side. As they made their way, Jesus glanced to his lover and wondered why part of him still wanted to fuck Muhammad. Of course, they were siblings, and his society expected siblings to fuck each other. It was the finest form of love a person could show to another.

Maybe Jesus had been on earth too long, but he wanted to stop having sex with his brother. Even though a part of him kind of wanted to hold him down, right now, and fuck the shit out of his ass.

He remembered when he was a kid at the age of a hundred and ten, when he reached the age when his people considered him a man. Before then he'd been celibate. As a right of passage, all of his elder siblings had to make love to him. In the event that there were no elder siblings, it would fall to the parents to aid their son or daughter. Four brothers and a sister introduced Jesus to the world of being an adult in one hyper-charged orgy of passion. No sexual adventure could ever match that, but Jesus thought that if he fucked Muhammad right now, this moment would at least hold its own. It had been so long, and Jesus' nuts were backed up.

Muhammad had always been the wickedest of his family. He'd learned his cruel ways from their father, the ruler of their home planet. How many societies had Muhammad crushed under his thumb? He probably couldn't remember all the people he'd killed. If he had his way, everyone on earth would be destroyed. Even Joe and his family. Hell, even that asshole, Antonio Santana.

Jesus stopped and gestured toward the pile of supplies. *There it is. There is more on the way, of course.*

Muhammad's eyes lit up, and he hovered around Jesus' offering, greedily admiring the materials that would go toward his next conquest, among other things. *You've done good, brother.*

Is it enough for now?

Muhammad came down for a landing and clapped Jesus on the back. *This is a bit less than I was hoping for, but we can make it work. Provided, of course, that you keep squeezing these wretches for all they're worth.*

They're good workers.

Muhammad almost snorted. *Workers? Please. Slaves are what they are. Speaking of which, how are things going with the revolts?*

Jesus smiled. *There are no revolts. I told you, love is the key to conquering the universe. Not fear.*

No revolts? You've got to be shitting me. There's no way they're not fighting back against you. Especially not stubborn assholes like these humans.

They did attack me at first, Jesus had to tell him. *But when I returned their violence with love, they fell under my sway. Make no mistake, I am the ruler of this world. But I'm a benevolent ruler. I love them, and now they love me back.*

Muhammad raised an eyebrow, then shook his head. *You really have gone native. If Dad were here to hear this garbage, he'd—*

He'd what? There isn't anything he hasn't already done to me. To us, for that matter.

I was going to say that he'd laugh at you.

That took Jesus by surprise. Their father was a harsh man, but he'd never laughed at them. Ridicule did not lead to the creation of great warriors, and laughing at someone was the ultimate insult where Jesus came from.

Muhammad rested his forehead against Jesus' and made a mental sighing sound. *Little brother, you still don't see the long game, do you. What do you think is going to happen when your precious planet has been bled white?*

Jesus' stomach went cold. He drew back from Muhammad, wide-eyed. *No. You can't. These are good people—*

It happens to everyone we conquer. When they're no good to us anymore, why should we keep them around? It's the humane thing to do, after all. Besides, I think your human friends would appreciate it. They're the ones who came up with the phrase "survival of the fittest."

Jesus couldn't control himself. He'd never felt such fury in his life, and it couldn't be contained. He lurched forward, screaming in his mind, and Muhammad sidestepped him, letting him drop to the ground.

Don't get up, little brother. For now I'm calling my companions, and we're going to take these supplies home. We'll be back in eight months for the next batch. Don't disappoint me.

143

Jesus pushed himself up and balled up his fists, ready to strike. Still, rage burned so brightly in him that he couldn't attack rationally, and Muhammad pushed him away without effort.

Last warning, little brother. I don't want to hurt you. Not today, at any rate.

Jesus didn't hear him. He launched forward again, and this time Muhammad cracked him with an uppercut. It felt like a boulder had struck him in the face as his head snapped back, and he felt himself floating away. Dazed, his fury finally calmed, he realized that Muhammad had struck him so hard that he'd pulled loose from the moon's gravity and was floating back to earth.

His eyes wanted to close, but he knew that if he passed out he'd forget to keep holding his breath, and he'd die before reentering the earth's atmosphere. He tried to correct his path, but since he hadn't pushed off the surface he had no control. Helplessly, he eased back toward earth, turning over and over as he went. He could watch as Muhammad was joined by the others in a cloaked ship and started loading up their supplies.

Finally Jesus felt himself getting caught in earth's orbit, so he had a force he could work against. He pushed against the grain and managed to gain control and momentum. His clothes burned away as he broke through into the earth's atmosphere and came down near Joe's farmhouse with a tremendous crash.

From there, he floated up to his bedroom

where he wrapped himself in a robe and fell back into bed. Muhammad could have torn him to pieces. What the hell would Jesus do when humanity's existence lost its value?

He couldn't think about it now. It hurt too much. His jaw throbbed with pain, but his heart felt worse. Gritting his teeth he turned a quarter of his blood to whiskey and felt it numbly take him away from consciousness.

CHAPTER 11:
THE CONFESSION

When Jesus woke up, groggy with a hangover, he knew what he had to do. He thought it might be best to keep it between Joe and himself, all things considered, but it had to be done.

He cured himself of his hangover and took a shower. Then he went down and surprised Ursula, who didn't know he'd come home the previous night. "I thought you were in Pennsylvania, looking over the coal mines," she said.

"Something came up," Jesus said. "I don't suppose you have any breakfast left over?"

"Coming right up."

Ethan and Allen were in school, and Joe was somewhere in Alaska, overseeing the removal of oil from previously protected lands, so it was just Ursula and Jesus in the kitchen. She didn't actually have leftovers, so she started cooking a new meal, but Jesus didn't notice. Instead he sat at the table and stared out at the yard, thinking. He barely reacted when Ursula placed a plate of eggs,

147

toast and bacon in front of him.

"You okay?" she asked.

He glanced up into her concerned eyes, and he felt sorry for ever manipulating her and the rest of her species. Maybe he should include her in this. Maybe . . . no.

"I'm all right. I just have to talk to Joe about something."

"He's pretty hard to get a hold of up there," Ursula said. "I've tried, and he's always out of the office. I guess you could try. Let me see if I have the number."

"In person, I meant," Jesus said.

"You're going to Alaska?"

"As soon as I finish breakfast," he said.

"Maybe I should make you some more eggs, then."

Later, after Jesus had finished Ursula's giant breakfast—even though it was closer to lunchtime by then—he got dressed in something a bit more comfortable and stepped outside so he could leave It was a good day with a high sun in a clear blue sky. Even up in Alaska, it would be fairly warm, at least for this time of year.

Jesus crouched down and then took off, sailing across America and over into Canada. His brothers usually travelled at nearly the speed of light, and Jesus *could* do it, if he pushed himself. He didn't want to do that today. For one, he wanted to admire the view. For another, he didn't really want to do what he had to do.

But, he had no choice.

A while later he came down outside of Joe's

office building. Workers with hardhats and orange vests trundled across the land, hard at work extracting oil from the ground. Everything had dark stains on it, and the gray overcast sky lent everything a stark clarity. Jesus could count the individual whiskers on every man's face.

He walked around to the entrance of the building, and the secretary greeted him with a warm smile. These days everyone greeted him with a warm smile. He couldn't help but offer it back.

"Is Joe expecting you?" she asked.

"No, it's a bit of a surprise. Sorry I couldn't call ahead, but this is pretty important."

"Sure. He's this way."

She led him past a few cubicles and into an office that had seen better days. Joe would have been the CEO of this operation if corporations still existed, but this was definitely not an administrator's office. Everything had a dingy quality. The carpet had worn almost all the way through, and an overcrowded bulletin board dominated one of the walls.

Joe's desk did not befit a CEO, either. It was a small metal table overcrowded with papers and coffee stains. He sat behind it now, looking at a map, not even looking up to see his visitors.

"Joe? It's Jesus. He wants to see you."

Joe looked up over the map and stuck a pencil behind his ear. "Jesus. I didn't expect to see you today."

"It's kind of an emergency," Jesus said.

"Something's come up, and I wanted to tell you about it."

"We're right on schedule, aren't we?" Joe asked.

"We are. It's not about that."

"Sounds like we might need some coffee. Hon, would you go get us—?"

"Sure," the secretary said.

"You might want to leave the pot with us," Jesus said. "We're going to be awhile."

"Of course."

When she came back with a tray, she placed it on the wobbly desk and poured them each a cup of coffee. Then, just as she was about to leave, Jesus held up a hand. "Would you please close the door? And let everyone know not to disturb us?"

She nodded and closed the door behind her.

"Uh-oh," Joe said. "I must be in trouble."

"Huh?"

"That's what my dad always used to say to me. The kinds of meetings where you have to close the door are never good. Am I fired?"

Jesus suddenly got it and laughed. Since his talk with Muhammad last night he hadn't been in a joking mood, and he didn't think he'd be able to recognize a joke. Still, his laugh felt empty even to himself. "Nothing like that. In fact, I think I'm the one who's in trouble."

"You?" Joe chuckled, sipping at his coffee.

"You know what St. Augustine said about confession?"

Joe, who only vaguely knew who St.

Augustine was, had no idea.

"'The confession of evil works is the first beginning of good works.' I think it's time I unburden myself, since I've . . . I've been less than honest with you. By far."

"How do you mean?"

Jesus drew in a deep breath and blew it out, hoping to quell his nerves. They still jittered under his flesh. "I'm going to tell you a story, and I don't want you to say anything. What I'm going to say will shock you. It will anger you. It might even disgust you. And in the end, it will scare you to your very core. But please, just let me say it, okay? Even if you don't believe it or you feel the need to object to it."

"If you say so," Joe said.

Jesus considered turning their coffee to whiskey, just to make this easier, but after a moment he decided not to. He had to do this with a clear head, and if it hurt too much . . . well, that was his penance.

He began.

CHAPTER 12:
JESUS STORY

I'm not Jesus Christ. My real name is Xathus, and I'm from the planet Xanadar.

Okay, look: This is going to go a bit better if you don't smirk at me. I know that sounds like some kind of crazy 'Fifties sci-fi movie to you, but it's true. It's my life.

All right, it's kind of funny, at least on the surface. But, by the time I'm done you won't be laughing.

Oddly enough, by your reckoning, I really was born approximately two thousand years ago. So I *could* be Jesus. But, I'm not.

My father is the ruler of Xanadar. He's King Xanadar, so I guess that makes more sense to you now. What kind of a megalomaniac would name his home world after himself? I always thought that was insane, but before he was king the planet was named after the guy who wore the crown before him. So there's a precedent.

Technically, I'm the seventh child of my father, who was a seventh child, himself. I know some cultures on this planet have superstitions about that kind of thing, but where I come from, it's fact. The seventh son of a seventh son is always special. Different. Sometimes they have super-intelligence. Sometimes it's super-strength. Some of them can even predict the future. Whatever the case is, they're always the most powerful beings in existence.

Try telling that to my dad.

In reality I'm the sixth child, so maybe that's why I turned out so lukewarm. The second eldest died in childbirth. He lived for five minutes, so I'm told. Sometimes I envy him. He didn't have to live on Xanadar.

Everyone on my home world is a warrior, even the women and children. We're trained from an early age to know how to fight, how to kill, how to *rule*. Many eons ago my ancestors realized the power they had and decided to not only make a super race of themselves but also to bring the universe to its knees. All other planetary societies existed to feed our needs.

I killed my first man at the age of five. I've killed so many more since, but you always remember your first. He dared to rebel against my father. He tried to save his own world, and dad slaughtered the guy's family in front of him. He saved this man for last because he wanted to turn him over to me. Everyone is clumsy with their first murder, and he figured I'd put the guy through hell before ending his life.

He was right. I made a mess of the poor man.

I never liked killing. I've ended the lives of countless beings. I've wiped out entire species. Once I killed an entire solar system. Just talking about it makes me sick. I-- I just can't stand the man I was. And still am, in some ways.

My siblings were all kill-crazy, especially my oldest brother Xanadar. I know, this is probably going to get confusing, but stick with me.

Anyway, they're all brutal, so much more than me. Xanadar—my brother, that is—took about a thousand years off once just so he could kill an entire galaxy, one creature at a time. He didn't wash the blood off, either. When he came home he had so much dried blood on him we barely recognized him. That was the first time I met him, by the way.

They all loved being the children of Xanadar, but not me. Killing people always turned my stomach. I did it, don't get me wrong. I'm just as guilty as they are. Mostly, I did it out of fear. Weaklings were not suffered to live on Xanadar, and not enjoying the destruction of entire races was considered very weak by my society's standards.

I also did it to fit in. I thought maybe I should be more like my brothers and sisters. I tried to follow the trends, I really did. I just became sicker and sicker as time passed.

Earth came to our attention maybe a thousand years ago, but you were all so primitive that no one gave a shit about you. We'd crush you under our heel whenever we got the chance. They put it on my "to-conquer" list. They considered it a goofy planet for a goofy family member.

I wanted to do a good job, so I started paying attention and discovered a shocking amount of culture here. Usually when it comes to alien planets, you get one dominant culture with maybe an underdog culture on the side. Not here. I couldn't even count the number of different societies that had grown here.

But one man fascinated me more than anyone else: Jesus Christ. I read all I could about him because I found that I identified with him a great deal. He came from a prideful society that wasn't satisfied until people who are different were dead or enslaved. Despite this, he preached love to people.

Granted, most people pretended to believe in him. They twisted his words around and used them to teach hatred and to enslave others. But still, the message was the same no matter who distorted it. *Love.*

I wanted to make that work, so I tried it out on a couple of planets. Wow. It did not work out. I'd tell you about Cava-12, but I don't even want to think about it.

I started to get a bad reputation among my family. They started making fun of me. I can take a joke. What I can't take is getting executed, which is the punishment for weakness. I played my process off as an experiment in strategy, which was completely acceptable to them.

But I think I'm really pushing it, here.

My family couldn't have cared less about earth until about seventy years ago, when we detected an incredible explosion coming from here. It was followed up shortly thereafter by another. Suddenly you had our interest.

When we studied your race anew, we realized that you'd developed weaponry so powerful that you could actually threaten us.

We had to have it. In fact, we do have it. We used your specs to build them. We actually found a planet made of Uranium-235, and we used it to completely annihilate countless galaxies.

But my family wanted everything your planet had to offer. My brothers started arguing over who would get to plunder the earth. None of them remembered that it had already been assigned to me, and my father had to remind them of it. You cannot imagine how furious they all were. Xathus gets this planet? That can't be right.

My father decided to use this opportunity to test me. We were going to subjugate your world, but a few things came up. We wound up going to war with another warrior planet from across the universe, and the earth got lost in the shuffle until recently.

Father warned me not to pull my usual shit, that if I screwed this up I'd suffer the greatest punishment our own kind can afford another. I nodded and said okay, but I knew I wanted to try out my "love" method here. They were inspired by a human being, so why not try it at home?

I figured that the message would be more

palatable if I arrived looking like Jesus himself. I preached love and awareness, just like him. I healed the entire world. I knew there would be problems at first, but I fixed them, didn't I?

For the first time since human beings started existing, this world is at peace. It is the perfect place in the universe to live. Believe me, I've seen a lot of this universe. There are a lot of hell-holes out there.

I'm sad to say that I didn't do it out of the kindness of my heart. I really did want to help my family get the supplies they needed, and this was the most humane way to get the job done. But while I was here I started falling in love with this place. With the people. With you. All of you. Joe, for the first time in thousands of years I have a family. A real family. I can't turn my back on that.

You're probably wondering why I'm telling you about all of this. If my plan wasn't so threatened I would have kept quiet. I would have let you all continue thinking I really was the second coming of Christ. I would have kept you all safe until the end of time.

But Xanadar—my brother—has endangered that. Do you remember the meteor that came down a while ago on your property? I lied. It was actually my brother. He came to check on me, and he came disguised as Muhammad, of all people.

There's that smirk, again. All right, all right, I admit it. I laughed when I first saw him, too. I don't even know why he did it. Did he think he was disguising himself? He doesn't have much of a sense of humor, so I'm completely lost on that one.

That doesn't change how dangerous he is, though. Ever since I came here he's been on me, trying to get me to bring the hammer down on the human race. He's angry that I didn't enslave you all and treat you like garbage. He kept giving me ultimatums about how if I fail, he'll take over and crush you all. But so far I've been able to keep ahead of him.

I saw him last night. He took delivery of the first batch of supplies, and he told me he'd be back for more, later. That doesn't surprise me, but he added something else that threw me for a loop. He said that when the earth is bled dry of its resources, he'll kill everyone on the planet. You won't serve his purposes anymore. And that's why I had to confess this to you. I've been a very bad person, and now I want to start doing good. This is the first step in that direction.

CHAPTER 13:
WHAT CAN BE DONE?

Jesus finally stopped talking, and he leaned back in his seat, waiting for Joe's reaction. His friend stared at him as if contemplating the secrets of the universe. Slowly, he worked a finger against his chin, tilting his head as he cleared his throat. "No offense, Jesus, but that is one of the craziest stories I've ever heard."

"You're a huge believer in the Bible," Jesus said. "You know how many crazy stories are in there. I also know that you believe in them all. I'm sorry, but evolution happened, and you're wrong about the Adam and Eve story. Job, Noah's ark, Lot's wives, all those are really crazy stories. What makes mine so much more crazier? Because mine is about aliens?"

"I remember when you first came here," Joe said. "You kept saying your mission here was to tell the truth. You came here to give us proof and eliminate the need for faith. Obviously, if you're not really Jesus Christ, you don't really look like him. Why not show me what you really look like?"

Jesus could detect a sardonic undertone to Joe's voice. Joe clearly still believed him to be Jesus. His lies had been so well-told that this man completely doubted the actual truth. He took a peek in Joe's head and saw that he had an image of a little green man in his thoughts.

"I'm not a little green man, Joe. I don't look all that different. I'm still humanoid."

"Okay, so let me see it, then."

Fuck it. Let's get this over with. Jesus closed his eyes and wished away his current visage. He tried imagining his original form, and he felt himself shrinking. The disguise faded away, and soon he sat before Joe in his true form, as Xathus.

When Jesus opened his eyes, Joe saw they were some kind of glittering golden color, like nothing he'd ever seen. Xathus's bald head gleamed, and his short but stout body looked kind of like a taller than usual fireplug. His teeth were pointy and razor sharp. He looked kind of human except for his arms; in their place were two thick, gigantic tentacles.

"Are you satisfied?" Xathus asked.

Joe swallowed, feeling an odd disgust with the creature in his office. Xathus's shape repulsed him, and he couldn't figure out why. Could it simply be his appearance?

"I know. No one likes the true form of a Xanadarian. We sicken everyone in the universe. It's some kind of magical effect, I think. I'm going to shift back to Jesus now, just for your comfort."

He did just that, and as soon as the

disguise was back in place, Joe grimaced. "All this time, you've been feeding us lies? Feeding *me* lies?"

"I'm sorry, Joe. I really am. I had to do it. I meant no malice by it."

"You only wanted us to give up our own freedom," Joe said. "I'll bet you'd vote Democrat, wouldn't you? Sounds like something the president would do."

"Joe, if I didn't do it, this planet would have been overrun by a real tyrant, someone who wouldn't give you the choice. He'd just take your freedom."

"That doesn't make things better," Joe said. "You're just as much of a monster as he is. It's just that you're more polite about it."

Jesus looked away from him, and he felt something burn in his eyes. He tried to hold on, but his throat seemed to grow bigger than his skin, and breathing became difficult.

"You have the gall to wear Jesus' face," Joe continued. "That's . . . that's true blasphemy. I can't believe I fell for it. I can't believe I helped you swindle the entire world. Do you realize that you've made a sinner out of me?"

The tears came forth, and Jesus couldn't stop them. They poured out of him in trembling waves, and he covered his face, hoping to hide his shame from Joe. Jesus had finally found a family, and he had to throw it away like this. Why couldn't he have kept his mouth shut? Why couldn't he have let the illusion continue?

No. It wouldn't have lasted. There would have come a day when Muhammad came back to murder all human beings, and Jesus knew he couldn't have lived with that. If his life continued he'd have to exist for at least fifty thousand more years. He didn't think he could live with something like that weighing his heart down for so long.

"No matter how much this hurts you," Joe said, "keep in mind that it hurts me a lot more."

"I know." Jesus couldn't keep the whine out of his voice. "I'm so sorry, Joe. Please believe me. I didn't mean to hurt you like this. I didn't mean to hurt anyone. I just wanted to stop the killing."

"Sounds like it didn't matter much," Joe said. "It sounds like we would have been wiped out no matter what happened. I can't believe I'm going to have to tell my family this crazy story. I'm going to have to tell them that we're all going to die. Ethan and Allen, they never got the chance to grow up and be men. I'm never going to have grandkids. This is . . . it's obscene."

Jesus sniffled, wiping at his eyes. "There's something we can still do. That's why I told you all of this. We can fight back. Xanadarians aren't invincible. Nuclear weapons can take them out. And if it comes down to a one-on-one situation, if you can figure out a way to separate our heads from our bodies, we'll die. My race is incredibly strong compared to yours, but if we fought against my brother and his soldiers, we could win."

"It's not likely, though. Is it?"

Jesus shook his head. "But we've got to try. There's a slight chance that your boys could grow up to be men. Wouldn't you risk anything on such a gamble?"

Joe finished off his coffee—it gurgled uncomfortably in his stomach and burned the back of his throat—and nodded.

"Can you ever forgive me?" Jesus asked.

Joe uttered an ugly, humorless laugh. "That's funny. Me forgiving Jesus. I . . . I don't know about that. But I think you helping us fight your own home planet goes a long way. The start of your good deeds."

"We have a decent chance," Jesus said. "My brother has no idea that we're going to fight back. We'll strike before they even know what's going on. We've just got to strike first and strike hard."

Joe nodded again. "Okay, then. What do we do?"

CHAPTER 14:
SEVERAL SOLAR
SYSTEMS OVER

Xanadar swiftly returned to Xanadar, the main capital of Xanadar, and immediately sought out Xanadar to give a status report. He left one of his friends in charge of unloading the ship and he leaped into the air, sailing toward the opulent Palace of Xanadar. It towered in the center of the city, where it shot into the sky and disappeared into the clouds above. On clear nights the entire swirling galaxy could be seen turning round and round at the pinnacle of its uppermost spire. Lit with neon, it made odd twists and turns over the city, something that wouldn't have ever lasted on earth. But here, the sheer unconventional beauty of it had reigned over the planet for millions of years.

Xanadar soared up to the top of the building, where even gravity started to weaken a bit, and when he reached the throne room portal he eased himself through and came to a gentle landing in the hall of his father. Pastels adorned the walls, and everything sparkled as if sprayed with a liberal dose of fairy dust.

The throne was a part of the wall. The back went up to the ceiling and curved into the wall. More neon highlighted the top and arms as well as the crown on his father's head. Two of Xanadar's aunts sucked the king's cock at the same time. There was enough room for both mouths on his gargantuan tool.

"Father, I have returned from earth," Xanadar said.

Xanadar didn't look up from his sisters blowing him. "Report."

"We got some supplies from Xathus. Not as much as we were hoping for but still a respectable amount."

"And what of my wayward son?" Xanadar asked.

"That's what I wanted to see you about, Father. I think he's been lying to us for a long time. I think he's Weak, and he should be destroyed."

"Explain."

Xanadar described what had happened on his recent meeting with Xathus on the earth's moon. Then: "He's clearly gone native. Not that he had very far to go. He's always been odd."

Xanadar gave his sisters a courtesy tap, and they stopped fellating him. Now, they each wrapped their hands around his cock and stroked him, until he gushed cum into their open mouths. They drank their fill and sucked him dry.

"Thank you. I'll come by later tonight and fuck the shit out of you. Both of you."

Xanadar's aunts descended from the throne and smiled at him as they walked past. He wouldn't have minded plowing the two of them alongside his father. He loved them both a great deal. But Xanadar didn't like sharing, so Xanadar would have to wait for later.

"What do you recommend, my son?" Xanadar asked. He wiped his dick off with his cloak.

"Send me back with an army. I want to capture Xathus and hold him prisoner. I want to make him watch as I enslave his beloved world. I want him to feel absolute pain as I take it from him. And then I want to kill him."

"No," Xanadar said.

"Father?"

"I like your plan, but you're not going to kill Xathus. I'm his father. I brought him into this world, and I will take him out. The pleasure of ending him goes to me. Understood?"

"Of course, Father." Xanadar bowed deeply.

"Good. When are you due to return to earth?"

"Three garns."

"Start planning for the attack. We want Xathus thinking that we're just there for our supplies, right on time. We don't want him thinking we're there to destroy the human race. The odds are in our favor, of course, but why give him any advantage? He's always been Weak, but he's not stupid. He's very

169

good when it comes to strategy."

"Yes, Father."

Xanadar left his father alone in the throne room and flew back out to the ship port so he could begin planning the raid immediately. Word got around quickly, and plans went into motion. He also gathered together his siblings, knowing that they'd want to be in on the action. They'd spent most of their lives despising their brother, and he had the feeling that all of them would jump at the chance to make him miserable.

Xanadar couldn't wait to see the look on Xathus's face when the end came. It gave him a hard-on.

CHAPTER 15:
THE BEST PLAN WE'VE GOT

Joe abandoned all of his own plans to start working on Jesus' plan. He couldn't do it by himself, so he enlisted the aid of the former president and all of her available connections, especially those at NASA.

Jesus, however, had his hands full, coming clean to the world. He contacted the people at Fox and got them to prepare a worldwide broadcast, and they had to do it quickly. He didn't know how long it would take Muhammad to return, and a lot of things had to be ready.

Jesus put on his best suit and groomed himself as best he could. He had felt that he could afford to wear rags, when he'd started his grassroots campaign to get everyone to buy into his story, but, now that he had to confess the truth, he knew he had to look sharp. People tended to be more forgiving to those who looked like they had their shit together. This one would be big, so he wanted to err on the side of caution. The last thing he needed was everyone turning against him when he needed them the most. There were still a lot of dangerous weapons in questionable hands, and he'd much rather have those resources used in fighting back against the Xanadarians. Jesus knew he could protect himself and maybe a few others from any violence committed by human minds, but if it was all wasted in an attempt to kill him, then he'd be less likely to win against his brother.

The odds were bad enough as they were.

After the preparations were all done, and the advertisements had all gone out, the studio turned its cameras on Jesus Christ and waited for his confession.

The red light went on, and the cameraman counted down on his fingers. On a screen in the background, a movie commercial wound down, and when it went black, the cameraman pointed to Jesus.

"Greetings to all, planet Earth. It's been a while since we had a heart to heart, and I'm sad to say that the circumstances of this one are . . . rough. I don't know how to lead up to it, so I'm going to just come right out and say it."

Unconsciously, he drew in a deep breath and let it all out. His nerves didn't stop jumping, though. Time to plow forward anyway. "I'm not who I say I am. I'm not Jesus Christ."

The cameraman peered around the camera, shocked. In the control room everyone stopped what they were doing to stare at the one screen that was live. In the makeup room

Brian Murphy, who had been flipping through news articles on his iPad, dropped the device and watched as Jesus bared his heart.

The entire world held its breath as Jesus told them all the truth. He started with his childhood and started moving up through his history and why he was here at all. More importantly, why he'd chosen to come to them as Jesus.

Then, just as he was about to explain the invasion they faced, Murphy burst into the studio hard enough to snap the door to pieces. It hung on by one hinge, swaying on the edge of falling off entirely, like a dislodged fingernail. Fuming, he stopped just at the edge of the camera's periphery.

"What is this, some kind of joke?"

In the control room the PD said, "What the fuck are you guys doing? Get full coverage. Whenever Murphy talks, go to camera three."

"But—"

"Do you want to go back to covering stupid pet tricks for a local affiliate?"

Jesus glanced over to Murphy, holding out his hands, palms up in supplication. "I'm sorry, Brian. I know this all seems crazy to you—"

"Crazy doesn't even fucking cover it. This has to be some kind of nightmare. How could you possibly say these things?"

"It's no joke, Brian. My real name is Xathus, and this is what I really look like." Closing his eyes, he concentrated enough to shift to his actual form.

173

Everyone stared wide-eyed at him. Not even Murphy could find anything to say. His mouth trembled, and he touched his lips, unable to believe he wasn't at home and dreaming this.

Jesus shifted back. "I know that was unpleasant to see, and I'm sorry. But I had to show you. Here, maybe this will help." He held up both hands, and a golden light emanated from the holes in his wrists. It formed a fog that slowly took shape to reveal a map of the universe. He manipulated it like an image on a tablet's touchscreen until the right galaxy was enlarged. He pointed at a planet. "That's my home. Xanadar. It's about —"

"Stop it," Murphy said.

"It's about a month away if you travel like we do. That's if one is traveling alone. Going by ship is a bit more time-consuming. It might take a half-year at most. Then—"

Murphy marched across the floor and slapped Jesus' hands down. The image dissipated with a short squeal. "I said, stop it."

Jesus wanted to object. They didn't have a lot of time to argue. For all he knew, Muhammad was already on his way back. He would probably have a fleet with him for more supplies. They had two hundred days at the very most, and Joe had a lot of things to get done in that time.

But, he reined himself in. "Okay," he said.

"How dare you?" Murphy said. "Have you forgotten where you are? This is the No BS

Room. What made you think you could waltz in here and tell all these lies in my studio?"

"I know it hurts," Jesus said. "I'm sorry. But at the time I thought it was necessary."

Murphy shoved his finger in Jesus' face. "You came here to give us the truth! You said you wanted to give us fact, not faith! And this is what you unload on us? A cart full of dung?"

It became harder to keep from lashing out, but Jesus somehow managed to keep himself in check. "I had my reasons, Brian."

"You came here to enslave us! To rule our planet!"

There. That did it. Jesus set his face. "To the second part, yes. To the first part? No. I don't have slaves. I have volunteers. But none of that matters now. If we—"

"Oh! Invasion and enslavement don't matter? Where do you get off telling us these things?"

"If you don't shut the fuck up, nothing will matter!" Jesus yelled.

"Are you threatening us?"

"No! But if you don't stop talking and start listening, my brothers and sisters will be here to lay waste to everything! You'll know what slavery feels like when they get here, and that's if you're lucky!"

Murphy paused, letting Jesus' words sink in. He let his finger drop, and he looked back at camera three, wondering what the rest of the world thought of this broadcast. Were they as stark raving mad as he was? Could this be the real truth this time? Would a warrior race soon arrive at earth to bend its occupants to their will?

Jesus caught his breath and managed to calm down a little. "That's right, planet Earth. There is a real invasion coming, and it's not going to be pretty. My father wants your resources, and he doesn't care who he hurts or kills to get them. When he gets everything you have to offer, he'll kill all of you. Every single one. Don't think that's an exaggeration. He's killed entire galaxies on a whim."

Murphy looked back to Jesus. "That can't be true."

"It is true. That's what I'm here to tell you all. We need to change direction, fast. In a few months they'll be here for the next batch of supplies. We need to surprise them. It will be tough. I imagine that we won't kill them all, and that some of them will survive to go back home, where they'll tell my father. He'll come with a really big invasion force, and that's not going to be easy to fight. It might even be impossible."

He touched Murphy's shoulder. "I'm sorry I lied to you. I didn't know this was going to happen. But, we need to work together if we have a chance against my family."

He turned back to the camera, and Murphy let his eyes drop, shuffling away from the broadcast. "Humans, please. I've made this a better world. It's almost been perfect, has it not? I've healed so many of you, and when was the last time someone committed a violent act here? Please, don't devolve to the way everything was before. If you start fighting each other, or even if you turn all your ire against me, you're doomed. We need to work together."

Then he started going into details.

About two hundred miles away, in the bowels of the White House, Joe let the room of geniuses and generals watch the end of Jesus' broadcast before clicking the off button on his remote. He turned to the crowd. "So, you can see we have a major problem."

One of the generals grimaced. "We let that pantywaist steal the world from us?"

"Believe me, I'm just as angry as you are," Joe said, "but we need to move past this. We have a war on our hands, and we're up against the deadliest enemy we've ever been known."

The general looked like he wanted to say more, but he remained silent. He glanced over to the former president, but he saw nothing in his ex-boss's eyes.

"I've gathered you all here so we can go over a plan," Joe continued. "As you can see, Jesus' brothers are—"

"Do we have to call him that?" This from one of the NASA guys, a puffy man named Fred. "I'd rather not, since that's not his real name."

"I don't think I could call him Xathus," a representative from Germany said. "That word feels too stupid in my mouth."

"We don't have time for this," Joe said. "He said that these people are almost impervious to anything we can throw at them except for nukes. Luckily we still have quite a few of those. Otherwise we'd have to remove their heads one by one, and I'm told that would be an almost impossible task."

"We can't set off nukes near earth," Nate, a scientist from MIT, said. "In our atmosphere it would be completely devastating. And, we can't set them off *near* our atmosphere because it would probably trap us in a veil of radiation we'd never recover from. To say nothing of EMP effects."

"And we can't fire them off in space." Someone from Oxford this time, a duffer named Ian. "Putting aside violations of the Outer Space Treaty, they just wouldn't work out there. They need air to work, and space is a vacuum. They would only destroy themselves and maybe anything the shrapnel runs into."

"Well, they *could* work," Nate said. "I think if you blew up a nuclear weapon in space, the device itself would bubble out in a circular plasma ball that would destroy everything it touches as it expands. The only problem is, I don't know if it would stop expanding, which would be bad news for earth and probably everyone in the universe."

"So anyone near it would be destroyed?" Joe asked.

"Anyone existing anywhere *could* be destroyed by just one nuke, theoretically," Nate said. "I'm talking the end of the universe, here."

"It's a moot point, anyway," Ian said. "We don't have a delivery system for such weapons in space."

"Well, I was thinking about that," Joe said. "The president says we have four space shuttles left over from the space program. Three of them are capable of flight outside our atmosphere: Discovery, Atlantis and Endeavor. Maybe we can fix up the Enterprise so she's space-worthy, too. After that, I figure we can put weapons on these things."

"Whoa," Fred said. "Do you realize how much research we'd need to do something like that? Trial and error?"

"Come on," Nate said. "Tell me none of your guys ever fantasized about weaponizing a space shuttle."

"Well . . ."

"They've all got ideas as to how it could be done," Nate said. "Just get them working on what they've already spent hours thinking about. I'll bet it can be done."

"Why?" Joe asked.

"Space battles are incredibly stupid," Nate said. "I'm sure it's okay for anyone on the offensive, but there is no way you can defend yourself outside of maneuverability. If anything breaches the hull, you're screwed. Maybe if we had shield technology, like in science fiction movies, but without that, anyone you send out there is probably not coming back. That's if they somehow evade being destroyed by firing their own nuke at the enemy."

"Out of curiosity," Klaus, the German, said, "what did you have in mind for these spaceships with nukes?"

"Jesus came up with a plan," Joe said. "Kind of an early warning system. He figured we could meet the Xanadarians at the asteroid belt between Mars and Jupiter. He thought it would be a good spot for an ambush, and if we were really lucky we could drive them off, at least long enough to recover and prepare for the bigger invasion. It might buy us enough time to build more ships and arm them."

Nate shrugged. "Hey, maybe I'm wrong. Maybe a nuke will work in space. Hell, if half of the things we know about these guys are true we might be screwed anyway. Might as well take them with us. If I'm right, that is."

"I may have a solution to your problem," Klaus continued. "It's one of our closest kept secrets—it goes back to Hitler's days—but I see no reason to keep it from the rest of the world now."

Every head turned toward Klaus, eagerly waiting. What could have possibly been so secret it had to be kept under wraps for more than seventy years?

"Werner Von Braun was working on weaponized space shuttles," Klaus continued. "We've had scientists working on the project ever since, but we don't have the proper equipment. I think if we had American resources we could finish them up in time to meet your deadline."

Nate stared at him. "You mean to tell me you have space war ships?"

The Chinese representative cleared his throat. "The Germans aren't alone. We have a number of our own design. We just haven't been able to test them. We couldn't do it without being noticed."

Nate and Ian exchanged a glance and then looked at Fred. "Why the fuck are we so far behind?" Nate asked.

Fred glared at the general and the president. "Someone thought defense spending was more important than funding space programs."

Joe could sense everyone was getting ready to start arguing. "This is great news. We might have a chance, after all."

"I'm told that it takes about a hundred and fifty days to get to Mars at this time of year," the general said, "That should get us there just in time to ambush these sons of bitches. Now that we have all of these ships at our command, I think victory is a given."

"What if it isn't?" Fred asked. "If those ships can't defend themselves, then what happens if the Xanadarian fleet tears through them like tissue paper? Do we have a backup plan?"

"We do," Joe said. "We have almost three thousand satellites in orbit. We figure that before the warships head off for Mars, they can stop by some of these things and weaponize them as a line of last defense."

Nate whistled. "If it comes to that, I hope to Christ . . . er, well. You know. I hope that I'm wrong about nukes in space."

"As it turns out," the general said, "we won't need the warships to make that stop."

"What do you mean?" Joe asked.

The general glanced at the former president, who nodded. "Well, during the Cold War we armed almost all of our satellites in case we needed to take down the Soviets from space."

"What?!" Nate almost shouted. "All this time—"

The Russian representative chuckled. "Great minds think alike. We did the same thing."

"Holy fucking shit!" Nate said. "Am I the only one who can't believe how psychopathic we all are?!"

"Don't knock it, son," the general said. "Chance favors only the prepared mind. Our psychopathic tendencies might have just saved the world."

Nate wanted to object to the misuse of Pasteur's quote, but it would be a waste of time. Besides, the general had made his point. A good one, at that.

"That's it, then," Joe said. "If they get through all of that, then it's down to ripping their heads off. Otherwise, this is the end of the human race. Any questions?"

"I have one," Ian said. "What does our friend Jesus think of our chances of survival?"

Joe considered lying to them, but what would that accomplish? "They're not good. But we've got to do something. We can't just let them use us and throw us away. We have to make a stand."

"Amen," the general said.

"Okay, that's it," Joe said. "You all

understand what we need to do. We need to get to work immediately. Pass word on to your subordinates, and keep me in the loop on your findings. I've got a few other things to coordinate, so if I can't be found you can report to my immediate advisor, the former president. All right?"

The group made a general sound of agreement.

"Good. Let's get to work."

CHAPTER 16:
THE BATTLE AT THE BELT

Jesus expected some kind of backlash from his broadcast—especially from the Israelis and Muslims—but nothing happened, much to his surprise. People understood the threat, and they were rightfully scared of the Xanadarians. They fell into line and got to work on Jesus' plan right away. The first month passed with some mishaps, but after everyone got the hang of their new job skills they made quick progress. China tested their space shuttles, and they worked perfectly. Germany coordinated with America to get their space shuttles ready for launch, and NASA worked with the military to get their existing space shuttles up to speed.

Nate made it his own personal mission to get the Enterprise updated and ready to fight. Being a huge *Star Trek* fan, it held a certain degree of significance for him, and he succeeded in record time.

While they did this, the few remaining astronauts from the space program went to work training soldiers, preparing them for what they could expect to deal with in space. Some of the toughest people on earth went for the job, and half of them failed to acclimate themselves to the rigorous standards of the program. The rest managed to master their new skill set, and soon the weaponized space shuttles were all ready to go, a new generation of trained astronauts in them, getting ready to use their new skills in a for-real space battle.

Of all people, Rich Bech made it through this new space program, and he did so well he was promoted to mission commander. He would lead the attack from the helm of the Atlantis.

"I've always wanted to go to space," he told Joe. "Ever since I was a kid. I wanted to get into the Air Force when I joined up, but my brother persuaded me to go with the Marines. I figured maybe some day I could transfer over, but when I lost my eye I thought I'd never get the chance. This is a dream come true for me."

"Don't forget, it *is* pretty dangerous," Joe said. "The chances that any of you are coming back at all are slim."

"That's all right," Rich said. "If getting killed means I helped save the human race, then it's worth it."

All of his fellow astronauts, be they American, German, Chinese or Russian, agreed with this sentiment.

As they approached the third month after Jesus' confession, the mission seemed more and more plausible. They knew they were ready. They had to be. If they waited any longer, the Xanadarian ships would beat them to the asteroid belt.

Preparations for launch began, and two weeks later, everything was set. Normally, the price for a worldwide launch of space shuttles would have cost more than all the money in the world. Now that money didn't exist, it didn't cost a dime. It *did* drain earth of nearly all of its resources, though.

Jesus thought it would be worth it. He *hoped* it would be worth it. Then again, even if it didn't work, the earth would be fucked anyway. Might as well tap the planet for all it was worth in an effort to save it.

All around the world, armed space shuttles launched at the same time. The insanely loud cacophony of explosions could be heard even in the remotest parts of the world. Forgotten tribes in the jungles of Africa and South America looked up, startled, and watched with awe as the sky filled with vapor trails, enough to enshroud the world in darkness for a day, making communication almost impossible.

Only three shuttles exploded. Three out of fifty-four.

Rich rendezvoused the Atlantis with the other ships near the moon, and they blasted off toward Mars as one fleet, ready to kick some alien ass.

Raina Lee, Rich's co-pilot, didn't have much of a sense of humor. She spent a lot of her time focused on her single-minded obsession: being the absolute best physical specimen she could be. She'd be damned if there was anything a man could do better than she could. A lot of the others thought she was a cold bitch, and that was fine with her. Time and time again, they'd tested her, and time and time again, she'd bested them. Rich was the only one she couldn't get a handle on; otherwise she thought, *she* would be mission commander.

She liked him, though. He was the only one who never made fun of her, and he actually supported her in ways the others wouldn't even dream of doing. If not for his two cents she wouldn't have gotten this much-coveted position on the Atlantis. They wanted to go with Jackson Briggs because he was a man. She'd taken Briggs down several times. She knew she could fold him in half nine times.

But for all she respected Rich, she couldn't understand the goofy bastard. She stared at the way his helmet had been painted. An odd circle with two bites out of it adorned each side, and he'd added tinting to his visor so it looked like he wore orange goggles. And even though they all faced certain death he had a childlike grin on his face.

He finally noticed her looking at him. "What?"

She pointed to his helmet. "What's that supposed to mean?"

"This? You mean to tell me you've never seen *Star Wars*?"

"Is that the one with those stupid teddy bears and the spears?"

"Hey, they're Ewoks, and they're vicious

fuckers. They eat their enemies. And anyway, that's the third movie. Or, well, the sixth, depending on how you look at it."

"It's either the third or the sixth. It can't be both."

"That's besides the point. The good guys fly around in these spaceships called X-Wings, and they wear cool helmets with these symbols on 'em."

Already Raina felt sorry she'd asked, but she'd started down this path. She might as well see it to the end. "Okay, but what does it *mean*?"

"It means I'm fulfilling a childhood wish," Rich said. "Not only am I finally in space, but I'm going to fight a space battle. And I'm one of the good guys. You have no idea how giddy that makes me feel."

"We're probably going to die."

"Well . . . yeah. That does put kind of a damper on it. But, we're all going to die someday, right?"

Raina stared at him, surprised by his utter lack of fear. She envied him that. Her nerves practically strained at her skin. She couldn't believe she'd fought so hard to earn this place on this ship headed for certain death. But then again she could easily believe it. She understood the part about being one of the good guys. All her life she'd strived to be on the side of right, and now that things seemed to be nearing the end she could think of nothing nobler than giving her life to save everyone else.

She had to know. She had to ask him.

Maybe he even had advice on how to let the fear go. "How do you do it?"

"Do what?"

"Supress the fear. Why aren't you afraid?"

He looked to her, and though he still smiled, there was something off about him. His eyes were a little too wide, and his mouth was a little too stiff. A mask looked through the visor at her. "I'm terrified, Raina. Every fiber of my being wants to turn around. Do you know much about World War I?"

"Just what I learned in school."

"Before that one, war was a grand adventure. Boys grew up wanting to get into the shit and battle their enemies, all that sort of thing. They even found romance in violent death. Glory. All of that. World War I changed all of that. It was an absolute meat-grinder. All of a sudden soldiers no longer thought it was fun. There was no adventure to be had. Of course the horror stories came home, so how do you think the world governments convinced young boys to fight for them?"

"Continuing the myth of the grand adventure."

"I need to pretend," Rich said, "or I'll go mad at the thought of my own death."

Raina thought an answer like that should scare the shit out of her. Instead she found a great deal of comfort in it.

Days turned into weeks. Despite their rigorous training, it took a long time to get used to space travel. Everyone had insomnia from zero gravity attempts at sleep, and as a result everyone tended to snap at each other. It was only after a month that exhaustion managed to help their bodies find an acceptable pattern.

The food didn't help. A couple of times, Rich almost turned them all around so they could get some cheeseburgers. They had condensed "burgers" in a tube, but it wasn't the same thing. He wanted—no, *needed*—to sink his teeth into a slab of meat, to feel medium rare blood ooze down his throat. And, of course, the very act of swabbing up ketchup with steak fries was too heavenly to leave his head.

By the end of the third month, they still weren't used to space living. Rich, who had grown up on a steady diet of science fiction, suddenly knew that human beings would never leave the earth. This was a mere five-month trip; he couldn't see people managing lengthy space travel like on *Star Trek*.

It didn't help that Briggs was an animal. He constantly told graphic stories about the pussy he'd gotten back on earth, and it seemed like he was doing it to try and turn Raina on, in hopes of getting laid one last time. She'd caught him watching her use the waste evacuator a couple of times. He'd flogged his dick like a monkey at the zoo.

The first time she caught him he displayed his manhood as if it were some kind of prize on a game show. "You want some of this prime beef?"

She glanced down at it. "The USDA would fail that little Slim Jim."

The words pierced his armor, but he played it off with a laugh. "It's only a matter of time, babe. I know you're not going to fuck a nerd like Rich. You and me? We're soldiers. That dummy's too busy playing Luke Skywalker to put it to you like you need it."

She wouldn't think of fucking either one of them. She kept the memory of her husband alive in her heart. He'd been a Navy SEAL. A mission had gone south, and half of his team got killed. From what she understood it was pure bad luck. A civilian had turned the wrong way down a road, and his headlights went across a field where Darren Lee and his men were hiding out. The enemy saw them, and the ensuing firefight left only three men alive.

Darren wasn't one of them.

She promised to never love another, that her only love now was for Uncle Sam. Not that this asshole would ever understand that. She tried to ignore him.

"Fuckin' dyke," Briggs said. "I'll fuck the rugmuncher out of you."

Cold rage built up in her, but she always remained a professional, no matter how rough things got. "Go play with your little dick, Briggs. It's the only thing you're good at."

She walked away, and behind her Briggs said, "It's just a matter of time."

Raina wanted to ball him up and kick him out the hatch, and she knew she could do it. Unfortunately she knew he'd earned his spot on the Atlantis just like Rich and Raina. She'd just been trying to get his goat with that comment about jerking it being the only thing he was good at.He knew how to fire the weapons on board, and he knew how to do it accurately. They were all trained in this, but he excelled to the point of almost being supernatural.

She thought about reporting Briggs, but she wasn't a rat. Besides, she had nothing to prove to anyone. She was better than him at everything. Protocol demanded it, and she obeyed the rules whenever she could, but turning him in meant that she couldn't handle him. Fuck that. A part of her couldn't wait for that shit weasel to try something physical.

It's just a matter of time, she thought. She didn't even know that her brain had parroted Briggs's last message to her, but she didn't need to be psychic. Soon, she started discovering cum stains on some of her belongings. Or on her spare clothes. Once, she had to clean out the waste evacuator because she thought it smelled like semen.

It came to a head during the fourth month. Rich had the helm and had ordered her to get some sleep. Raina couldn't argue much; weariness almost blurred her vision. She told him she'd be gone for a couple of hours at most, and then he could take a break. She passed Briggs on her way back, and he'd looked busy checking buttons and dials. Thinking back, she knew he was pretending. He'd peered at the readouts a bit too intently.

At the time, she didn't think about it.

Instead she went to the back of the ship and strapped herself down, so she wouldn't float around while trying to sleep. Even this late into the trip, she couldn't easily find slumber, but her body had become reasonably acclimated to the atmosphere. It took her maybe twenty minutes before her exhausted mind allowed her to sleep.

Raina dreamed about her father for the first time in years. He'd been an old school tough guy who'd wanted nothing more than a son so he could pass on his knowledge and skills. He didn't want his kid to be some politically correct hippie. No, sir.

He never did get a son. Instead he got Raina, and her lack of a penis didn't seem to deter him from his plans. He raised her up to be a soldier from the very moment she could walk. By first grade she could shoot the dick off a fly at twenty paces.

He'd died in his forties of a heart attack. Too much cheese with every meal. She missed him so much that she still couldn't imagine him as a dead man.

Now she dreamed about the first time she'd brought a boy home. Everyone in the family had been terrified of what would happen. It was generally assumed that he would shotgun the first boy who so much as asked her out. This wasn't great for the confidence of the boy in question, who nearly pissed himself at the thought of meeting her old man. Even she'd bought into this way of thinking.

Everyone was wrong. Her father was polite to the boy, and later, when she asked about his attitude toward her dating someone, he didn't hesitate. "I'm not an expert when it comes to relationships. Your mother ran things in that department. But I raised you right. I trust your judgment."

Four years later she met Darren, proving that her father had been right.

But in her dream, her father had just finished his speech, and at that point the boy —Jimmy Erickson, a cute baseball player with a soft head of strawberry blond hair— turned into Jackson Briggs, leering at her, helicoptering his dick.

"Just kiss it, bitch," Briggs said. His teeth were clenched.

She actually felt something press up against her lips, and an invisible man grabbed one of her breasts, squeezing roughly at her.

It felt too real. A voice deep down in her mind knew it couldn't be real, that this had to be a dream. She tried to force herself awake, but as she opened her eyes she saw Briggs crouched over her, his eyes staring and intent as he breathed heavily. One of his hands touched her breast gently, as if trying not to wake her. His other hand held his dick, which was cautiously pressed against her lips, the tip slightly pushing them open.

"Just kiss it, bitch," he whispered.

She recoiled, pushing him away. He yelped as he fell back, but not because it hurt. In zero gravity it was hard to fall anywhere. Fear alighted in his eyes, and she knew that the only pain he felt was the pain of being discovered.

Raina felt the urge to beat the shit out of him. She wanted to blacken his eyes, but she knew he'd need those when they got to the asteroid belt. She also wanted to bend the offending hands backwards until they snapped like a bundle of sticks, but again he would need those, too.

Then she saw his erection, standing proud despite his fear. It was a bit bigger than she gave him credit for, though she would never let him know that. It wouldn't be for much longer, anyway.

"I'm sorry," he said. "I thought you were sleeping."

She didn't hesitate. Her foot lashed out and connected where the root of his cock met his ball sack. Something crunched, and he wailed until he ran out of breath. He couldn't seem to breathe in, so she stomped his dick again. Not only did it wilt, it actually snapped in half, almost like a boomerang.

He blacked out. Considering the tiny thread of blood oozing from his dickhole, it was probably for the best.

Raina didn't like having to report the incident to Rich, but she had to. She expected her commanding officer to tear her a new one, considering Briggs's importance. She was ready to defend herself by saying that she'd restrained herself from damaging the important bits—it wasn't like Briggs needed his dick to fire nukes at aliens—but it turned out she needn't have worried.

Rich surprised her. "Don't think I haven't

noticed his inappropriate behavior. I have, and I've recorded it in the captain's log. If we somehow survive this he'll be getting court marshaled at the least."

"Out of curiosity, why didn't you say anything?" she asked.

"Probably the same reason you didn't, either," Rich said. "You can take care of yourself. Something tells me that he's never going to try anything with you again."

Things got unpleasant when they had to administer first aid. Rich told Raina to take the helm while he put some gloves on and went to work. Setting the broken dick was probably the last thing he wanted to ever do with his life, and judging from how Briggs screamed the patient agreed on a level more personally than Rich could ever imagine.

Things were more tolerable onboard the Atlantis after that. Briggs wanted Raina's blood, but Rich managed to convince him that it would be in no one's interest for that to happen. "Besides," Rich said, "if anything happens to her, I'll make sure this broken dick is the least of your worries. Do you understand me?"

Grudgingly, Briggs understood. He avoided Raina at every opportunity.

Near the end of the fifth month, they arrived at Mars ahead of schedule. Now that they could get the lay of the land, they could strategize. He called a conference of the Chinese, German and Russian commanders—Aiguo Cheng, Wesley Van Hoorst and Vasili Dostoyevskivich, respectively—and started talking about what they needed to do. Thankfully, all of them spoke English. Rich could never get his head around how many people in other countries learned English as a matter of routine. He took two years of Spanish in high school and could only remember the curse words now.

The consensus was that they had to stay on the sunny side of Mars, away from the rest of the solar system. It wouldn't be very easy to hide among the asteroids for their ambush. However, they couldn't put all their eggs in one basket, either.

Van Hoorst said, "Our ships are the smallest and most maneuverable. I'll take them into the asteroid belt and hide out there, waiting for the enemy to come through. Then, when their fleet is through, the rest of you spring out from behind Mars and attack. We'll close in behind them and blindside them. If we work things right we might even survive to get a hero's welcome back home."

Cheng consulted a few maps and graphs. Then he shared the screen of his iPad and made a circle on the map. "We lucked out, gentlemen. It just so happens that Ceres is here. It's the biggest of the asteroids. It's technically a dwarf planet, and its fortuitous presence means we can easily hide some of Commander Van Hoorst's ships behind it."

Rich nodded. "That's close to one of the three paths of least resistance the Xanadarians are going to use. It couldn't be better. But it looks like an obvious place to set a trap. Do you think they know that?"

"Almost certainly," Cheng said. "I think their arrogance will blind them to it. They would never imagine us heading them off like this."

"Jesus said they know we've left our planet," Dostoyevskivich said. "Such a trap might not be far from their minds."

Rich looked at the other two paths. No, the one past Ceres was the best bet. Why risk getting your fleet fucked up by asteroids when you didn't have to? "I'll have to agree with Commander Cheng. These guys are walking, talking, flying hunks of hubris. I think we'll get the drop on them. We might not have the strength to win, but we'll put a dent in them they won't forget."

They discussed tactics for a while longer before they split up to take up their positions. From here they settled in, waiting. Rich had brought a deck of cards with him, and he played War with Raina. Briggs ignored them all and spent most of his time alone and typing on his tablet.

Back on earth, Jesus, who for the past few days had heightened his senses in preparation for Muhammad's return, felt something tickle at his consciousness. He couldn't extend himself much farther, but he thought he felt Muhammad approaching the asteroid belt from the Jupiter side.

Jesus flew down to Houston and had them send this message to Rich: "It's time. They've reached the belt. They'll be there any day."

Five minutes later, Jesus got the answer: "We're ready and waiting to kick some ass."

Two days after they received the warning, Rich heard from Van Hoorst: "Heads up, Commander Bech. They're here."

The German sent a video feed over. Rich couldn't believe the size of these ships. He imagined they were about as big as Star Destroyers in the Holy Trilogy. If this was a fair fight, they'd stand no chance against these guys.

Luckily they had surprise on their side. And nukes.

"Raina, Briggs, I think it's time to get in our suits."

"What good will that do?" Briggs muttered. "If this hull gets breached, the loss of air pressure alone will probably kill us. Even if it didn't, do you think we can survive outside of this ship? What's to stop these assholes from killing us as we float around like retards in space?"

"We fight to the last drop," Rich said. "I thought you knew that, soldier. They'll kill us for sure, but we're here to make them feel the hurt. I'm not going down without giving these motherfuckers a fight."

"Amen," Raina said.

Briggs didn't say anything else. He just fastened his helmet in place. No one locked down yet, but they got locked down enough so that all they had to do was flick a switch and they'd be able to survive in their suits.

"I think that's all of them," Van Hoorst said on the communicator. "I can see them approaching Mars pretty quickly. They should be there in about five minutes.

Commander Bech, I would recommend that you give the order to attack in exactly three minutes and twenty seconds. After that, we might lose the element of surprise."

"Affirmative," Rich said. "All shuttles, please prepare for movement and stand by for my command to attack."

Raina started powering up the ship. From inside, it sounded like a thousand engines revving. Outside, however, no one could hear a thing.

Rich stared at his clock, counting down the seconds. Raina tried not to think about what would happen next. She'd been trained well, and she hoped her instinct would take over, that she wouldn't even have to consider her movements.

Briggs just wished he could have gotten his dick wet one last time. Hell, it would have been nice to jerk off one more time, but he couldn't get hard anymore, not since Raina stomped him. Maybe death would be for the best. He didn't want to go on living in a world where he couldn't use his dick.

Rich thought about nothing. His entire world was made up of those numbers.

They had ten seconds left, and Rich took a deep breath. Held it. Let it out at the five-second mark. Sweat stood out on his forehead, and he trembled slightly. Four. He thought about Jesus and all the good he'd done, even though he'd been a charlatan. Three. It would be nice to see the earth one more time, to enjoy a cold beer on a hot summer day. Two. It would have been nice to kiss a beautiful woman one more time. It would have been best if it was Jenny Bretton, his high school sweetheart. One. Holy shit, this was it. No turning back. Time to face the end like a man, and hurt these evil sons of bitches.

Zero.

"Front wave! Attack!" he bellowed into the communicator. "Attack! Back wave, stand by for further orders!"

The ship lurched as Raina nudged the controls, pushing the Atlantis out and around Mars, weapons ports aimed at the invading horde.

In that moment, peering out through the monitor at the front of the shuttle, Rich felt suddenly overwhelmed with awe. He couldn't count how many ships were incoming, but there had to be thirty or so of them, all big motherfuckers. His chest hitched, and his dick shrank, and the certainty that they were all fucked came over him.

He had to force logic back into his head. The enemy had bigger, more powerful ships, but the earth warriors had surprise. They had the second wave. At the very least they outnumbered the enemy.

Rich didn't have a hope of surviving this. He knew now that hope was fruitless. But he knew their sacrifice would not be for nothing. They'd get killed, but he knew they could get half the fleet before they knew what hit them. Maybe only three of those behemoths would even make it to earth.

On one of the Xanadarian ships

Muhammad stared out the window, shocked. "This can't really be happening, can it?"

Puzzled, he continued looking at the earthlings in their ships. Never in a million years had he expected something like this from people that stupid. That spineless. That inefficient. His brother had really worked them up, hadn't he?

It would be for nothing, of course. Their evasive maneuvers would be a bit sluggish at this point, so the earthlings would definitely take out a number of their ships. However, it didn't matter. Xanadarians could survive in the vacuum of space, just so long as they got a chestful of air first.

Time to make short work of these talking apes.

In the Atlantis, Briggs peered into his monitor at the feed outside. One by one, the enemy ships lit up as other weapons officers on other ships locked in their targets. Briggs tapped one of his own. "Target locked, sir."

In Rich's earpiece he heard other ships check in with the same message. When he'd heard enough, it was time. He said, "Fire at will!"

Briggs hit a red button, and one of their nukes blasted off toward its target. Rich watched as it floated away, propelled by its boosters. The moment of truth. He really, really hoped this wouldn't be the end of the universe.

The Xanadarians seemed to know that they'd been targeted, and they began shifting their trajectories. Their movements were sluggish, and one of them bashed into an asteroid. Even though the asteroid crumbled, the ship seemed to flatten. It didn't seem to hurt the people inside, though. Even from this distance Rich could see them crawling out into space. Jesus had warned them that his people could survive outside of a ship. He just hoped the nukes would nail them before they managed to get over to this side of Mars. He knew for certain they wouldn't be able to fend off an unarmed attack from them. Jesus had also told them that Xanadarians would be able to punch holes in their shuttles. Not good.

The first nuke connected with an enemy ship, and a molten ball started to expand at a rapid rate. Just like the kid from MIT had said. Oh, fuck.

One by one, the nukes exploded in space, turning into white hot plasma balls that kept expanding. The bombs cut through the Xanadarian ships just before they became a part of their mass. Each one spread out for five miles, until they started touching each other, becoming one giant, all consuming ball of destruction.

And it didn't stop expanding.

"Fuck!" Rich yelled. "Fuck fuck fuck fuck FUCK!"

Raina looked over to him. "Fuck," she said.

Briggs couldn't even speak.

Five minutes later, down on earth, Nate stared at the video feeds from Mars, and he wanted to cry. "I should have told them not to do it," he said. "Now I've caused the end of all existence."

The general squeezed Nate's shoulder. "Take it easy, kid. At least we took those bastards out with us."

That gave Nate no comfort whatsoever.

Just as the footage had made it back to earth, a miracle happened. Rich couldn't believe it as he watched the balls reach a diameter of seven miles each, and then they stopped. They had almost reached a blinding brightness, but now they dimmed and froze in place. One of the balls had consumed the free-floating Xanadarians, and their dead, agonized faces and limbs poked out of the cooled surface, ghosts forever trapped in that one moment like shadows in Hiroshima.

When Nate saw it he gave a sudden cheer that startled the general. "What was that for?"

"We're going to survive!" Nate cried. "They were on the other side of Mars, so the ships must have been shielded from the sun!"

"Okay, well, what does that mean?"

"The space around the dark side of a planet is way cooler than the sunny side," Nate said. "The cold must have frozen the explosions. Which means . . . holy shit!"

"What?"

"We can't fire the nukes from the sunny side of earth when the aliens get here. We have to get them on the dark side."

The general still didn't understand, but he knew when to trust smart people. He whipped out his cell phone and relayed his new orders. Above them, satellites slowly changed their trajectory in preparation.

By Mars the balls of cooled radiation drifted back and fell into the gravitational pull of the asteroid belt. In that moment Rich realized that they only had three enemy ships left unscathed, and they were angrily making their way forward. Weapons started expanding from their hulls.

"Pick new targets and fire!" he shouted. "Back wave! Make your move!"

They weren't fast enough. Cylindrical objects blasted from the remaining ships, and they looked oddly familiar. They looked almost like—

"Fuck!" Briggs shouted. "You see that, commander?"

"They look like—"

"Nukes! They're nuking us!"

"Fire on them," Rich told him. "Raina, prepare for evasive maneuvers."

Earth ships fired more nukes and tried getting out of the way. Van Hoorst's ships came from behind, blasting with complete abandon.

Unfortunately, the Germans were too close to the Xanadarians, and the Xanadarians had weapons mounted to the backs of their ships. More molten balls formed in space. Von Hoorst's ships vanished almost immediately. Another Xanadarian ship joined them.

Muhammad roared at the helm of his ship. Never in the history of Xanadar had his people suffered such a great loss. He figured he could take half of the earth fleet with him, and he smiled as the Enterprise turned into plasma. He knew they had one more chance.

They had two ships left. That came out to about fifty Xanadarians, including himself and his father. If he had it figured right, the earthlings didn't have short range weapons. If they could only get close enough to them, they could easily tear their ships apart with their bare hands.

He flipped on the communicator. "Abandon ship, everyone! Immediately. And then head for the earthlings as fast as you can! We can't take another nuke hit, but we can sure take them apart close up!"

Everyone filled their lungs with one final breath and waited as their ships decompressed. When it was safe enough they went out the hatch and soared across space, dodging nukes and balls of radiation, intent on reaching the earth warriors.

Rich saw them and knew this was the end. The final two Xanadarian ships were gone, and enough nukes had taken out most of their own fleet. He could still see about ten earth ships, and one of them was the Endeavor.

"Target the individuals and fire," he said into the communicator. "If they get over to us, we're fucked. See if you can concentrate fire in one area and create an impassable section of space. Can we do that?"

"It'll be tricky," Briggs said, "but it's all we've got."

He coordinated with the remaining weapons officers, and before long they launched the final payload on each ship.

It was almost in time. About twenty of the Xanadarians got through before the nukes detonated, wiping out the rest of their number.

"Well," Briggs said. "That's that."

"Yeah," Rich said. "We did good, though. I think we saved the world."

A Xanadarian flew into the Endeavor so hard he cut through the entire ship and came out on the other end. The hull collapsed, and they could see pieces of the crew floating out through the holes. Buzz Aldrin, a badass tough guy to the very end, managed to keep up with the others in training, enough so he'd earned a seat as commander of the Endeavor. Now they watched as pieces of him drifted out into space.

"We're so fucked," Briggs said.

Raina squinted. "Is that Elvis?"

Rich looked over and saw that the Xanadarians had all chosen earth disguises. He could see Muhammad as well as Buddha and Thor and Zeus and so many others, including Elvis, Ronald McDonald and Frankenstein's monster.

And then something clicked in Rich's head. He couldn't help but laugh.

Raina looked out at doom rushing towards them. "I could sure use a joke right now, Commander."

"These assholes think we worship Elvis and Ronald McDonald. Like, they're gods or something."

Raina cracked a smile. Then she started giggling uncontrollably. Rich lost it completely and guffawed behind his Star Wars visor. Only Briggs remained silent. He saw that Muhammad was coming directly for them. Quickly he turned on the communications feed back home.

"Houston, please. This is Briggs. I've got a son. His name is Jeffey. He's only three. You've got to tell him I love him. And tell my cunt of an ex-wife that I'm not paying her any more alimony!"

Muhammad's furious face grew larger and larger in the window frame. Rich and Raina stopped laughing. "It's time," she said.

All three locked down the seals on their suits. In that moment Rich realized that the Xanadarians shouldn't have survived the decompression of their ships. How? And then, it came to him in a flash.

"Raina! We still have a chance! Decompress the ship!"

She didn't hesitate. She flipped the switch immediately, and air hissed out of the cabin. Outside, Muhammad slowed down so he could peer through the glass. He grinned and waved at them.

Raina glanced to Rich. "It's been an honor to work with you."

"You, too," he said. They shook hands.

"You guys suck," Briggs said. "Especially you, Raina."

She didn't give him the satisfaction of responding. Instead she unclipped her seat belt and started floating. Rich did the same.

And Muhammad punched through the glass. There was still a bit of air left inside, but it wasn't enough to cause the ship's collapse. Muhammad noticed, and nodded at the unexpected intelligence of these people.

He ripped the ship in half, and all three occupants pushed off, floating toward him, fists balled in their gloves.

Rich knew that these guys survived in space by holding their breath. He hoped he could get a good gut punch in, just enough to get this guy to lose his air.

You'll never make it, a voice said in his head.

Looking at Muhammad, he knew the thought had come from him. Defiantly, Rich thought back at him: *Fuck your mother.*

Muhammad didn't get it. The human clearly meant it as an insult, but making love to his own mother for the first time had been one of the happiest moments of his adolescent life. It had to be some kind of earth colloquialism.

The three astronauts threw their fists at Muhammad in unison. Unfortunately, nothing moves very quickly in space, and their punches felt like feathers on his body. Unlike them, though, he could pack a wallop without moving much. He knocked them all away and went after the closest first: Briggs. Muhammad tore his suit open with one casual hand. Briggs had seen this coming and drew in a deep breath, hoping it would buy him some time.

Which was the one thing he was trained *not* to do back on earth. As soon as his suit opened and he lost pressure, his lungs popped and he died without realizing what had happened.

Raina next. Muhammad clamped his hand down on her helmet, sticking his fingers through, and yanked up, popping it off her suit completely. Raina pushed all of her breath out. Coldness filled her suit immediately, and her ears popped.

But, she was still alive, and she knew that she had maybe a half a minute of life left. In all likelihood she would only have fourteen seconds of consciousness left to do something.

She lunged forward and buried her teeth into Muhammad's throat, getting a mouthful of windpipe. Worrying her head back and forth as hard as she could, she tried to pull back.

It was no good. Her teeth weren't strong enough to penetrate Xanadarian skin. Still, she didn't give up. She grabbed Muhammad's shirt and held tightly, still trying to bite out his throat.

Muhammad couldn't believe it. First of all, he'd been surprised that this one was a woman. Very few cultures allowed their women to fight, which he thought was a big mistake, considering how strong his mother and sister were. Yet here was a tough female earthling, fighting as hard and long as she could. He'd never seen someone with so much battle in them, much less a woman from a non-Xanadarian race.

He almost respected her for it. Almost.

The fight went out of her eyes as she lost

consciousness and her teeth slipped away from him. He'd waited for this to happen in order to show a form of mercy, an unusual thing for him. As soon as she'd passed out, he reached for her head.

"No!" Rich screamed. He paddled his arms in space, trying to get back to Muhammad, but the momentum from when he'd been knocked back was too much to overcome. He watched, helpless, as Muhammad squeezed Raina's head until it popped. Skull fragments and brain matter spiraled away from her, and out into infinity.

Rich felt defeated as he watched Raina's body float away. Three earth ships remained, and as despair crept through Rich's guts, the Xanadarians tore them to pieces.

Muhammad approached Rich and grabbed him by the biceps. They stared at each other through their visors, hatred boiling between them.

Well, we fucked you up bad, Rich thought.

Muhammad's eyes narrowed. *Fuck your mother*. Hoping he'd used the phrase right so as to hurt this earthling. Then he lifted his hand, one finger extended.

Rich knew what was coming. Contrary to his training, he drew in half a breath. He had one final thing to do.

Muhammad's finger touched Rich's visor, and then he gave it a light—for a Xanadarian —tap. The visor shattered, and Rich could feel his lungs buckle. He didn't have enough air for them to pop. With his last ounce of willpower, Rich spat in Muhammad's face.

The spittle didn't travel very fast, but Muhammad didn't expect it. Saliva rolled across his face in one big gob.

On Xanadar, the highest form of insult is to spit into the face of a fellow Xanadarian. The ultimate form of disrespect. Muhammad didn't hesitate to retaliate; he punched Rich in the chest hard enough for his fist to come out the other side. Rich's exploded heart floated out his back, and he died with a defiant grin on his face.

Elvis—Xanadar's father, Xanadar—flew over to Muhammad. *Good work, son. You'll make a great king when I'm gone.*

Muhammad pulled his hand out of Rich's chest and sent the corpse on its way. He stared after it, watching as it came into the gravitational field of Mars. Soon he would hit the planet's atmosphere, and his body would burn up into ash.

Fuck him.

Let's finish these cocksuckers off, he said.

Elvis nodded, and they led the other Xanadarians towards earth.

CHAPTER 17:
THE BATTLE OF EARTH

Five minutes after the destruction of the final ship near Mars, Jesus turned away from the wall of monitors. Each one now displayed blank blue screens. He looked around the room full of people—from NASA, the military and the top schools of the country formerly known as America.

"It takes them thirteen minutes to get from there to here," Jesus said. "The message ate up five of those minutes, so we have eight minutes before the attack. General, have your team ready."

The general nodded and went to work. Everyone scrambled about in preparation for what could be their final stand. Nate looked over to Jesus. "Our guys did a better job than we thought they would."

Jesus nodded. They could comfortably fit about twenty-five Xanadarians per ship. He'd counted thirty ships in the fleet. Considering that earth only had to face about twenty of his people,the odds were certainly better, but all it took was one Xanadarian to destroy a planet. The thought left an uncomfortable feeling in his stomach.

At the halfway point, the Xanadarians could see their destination ahead, a tiny blue ball highlighted by the blazing sun behind it. Elvis, the oldest and strongest of the bunch, could also see further than the others. He could see the satellites at this distance, and he knew what the earthlings had in store for them. As they soared ahead, he relayed his instructions to his men. Then he concentrated on Jesus. Without even trying, he found his son in Texas. Quickly, he picked through Jesus' brain, looking for someone he loved more than anyone else. He knew Jesus had grown to love his subjects, and he wanted to find the one whose death would hurt Jesus the most.

There! Joseph John McDonald, who was currently at home with his family, hoping to protect them from the Xanadarian invasion. As if a human could do that without the help of a nuke.

The Xanadarian force moved closer and closer, until he knew he had earth's attention. He could feel their cameras on him.

Follow my plan, he told the others. *Son, you're in charge. I've got business to attend to.*

Muhammad understood, and he took the lead, as Elvis jetted off in another direction.

On Earth, Jesus kept his telepathic feelers out until he could see his people on the satellite feeds. Now that he no longer needed to keep tabs on them, he closed his mind off.

Xanadarians rarely fought against each other, but when they did it was a matter of survival to cut off their minds from the rest of their species. If they didn't, they would read each others' thoughts, and the fight would end in a stalemate with no way for anyone to gain the upper hand.

He turned to the former president. "All right, I'm going to the other side of the planet to meet them. From here on out, you're in charge. Good luck."

"You'll need more luck than us. If they get past the nukes -- and judging how the footage went they probably will -- we're doomed."

"Remember what you saw," Jesus said. "Have them concentrate the nukes like the space shuttles did. It won't get them all, but it won't be a waste of time."

They shook hands, and Jesus took off, following the curve of the earth east. Then, just as he crossed over to the side where it was still night, he felt his entire body cool. In the distance, he saw the Xanadarians with his own eyes. He stopped, hovering so he could watch and see what the nukes would do.

The general watched footage of the approaching Xanadarians. They all seemed clustered together. A perfect target. He waited for them to get a little closer before he told his men to lock in on their targets. The enemy was still beyond the moon—far enough so that the plasma balls wouldn't get stuck in earth's orbit—when he gave the order to fire.

The satellites sent out their nuclear

weapons, and at that moment the Xanadarians spread out at hyper-speed and flew around the massive amount of missiles passing by them. The bombs detonated, and giant molten balls erupted in space.

To the general's horror, they only took out one measly Xanadarian. The Xanadarians descended all over the planet and started wreaking immediate and savage havoc.

Jesus couldn't believe what he'd just seen. He knew the nukes wouldn't get all of the Xanadarians, but he'd expected more than one casualty on their side. At the very least, he thought Muhammad would seek him out and confront him. His brother liked to gloat, and the situation certainly called for it.

No, Jesus would have to find Muhammad, but he didn't want to open his mind, not at this stage in the battle. He'd have to do it the old fashioned way. He could still see the vapor trails his people had left through earth's atmosphere. He picked the closest and followed after it.

On the sunny side of the earth, Rev. Austin Potts knelt in his rectory, praying. He hadn't been the same since Jesus' confession. It hurt him deep down. Ever since Jesus had arrived, Rev. Potts thought his lifelong faith had finally paid off. In his darkest moments, when he thought a little too much about the boy who lived across the street and liked to play soldiers in the front yard while bent over, he had doubts. How could God put those thoughts in his head? The only reasonable answer was that God didn't exist.

Yet his training always kept him in check. He never acted on his impulses, beyond going back into his walk-in closet and feverishly masturbating in the darkness, away from anyone who might discover him.

When he met Jesus, he knew he'd been right to stay the course for these past thirty years. And, when Jesus took the evil from his heart? For the first time since little Austin had been raped by his father's best friend—the non-familial uncle—he no longer felt self-revulsion. He didn't feel "wrong." All his fear and loathing dissipated.

He felt free.

When Jesus revealed the truth about himself, Rev. Potts's first response was anger—not just at this imposter—but also at himself. He had fallen for it. His mentor had always taught him that even the devil could quote scripture, and now he found himself taken like a fool.

But . . . the alien who called himself Jesus really *did* fix him. That's what kept Rev. Potts strong in these dark times. The stranger couldn't be all that bad, could he? Sure, he'd been dishonest, but in the end he'd done good, more good than anyone in the history of earth had ever done.

They needed to be strong in order to face the invasion, and Jesus had done that.

It didn't stop Rev. Potts from praying, though. They needed a miracle. Hands clasped together, eyes closed, he whispered softly to a God he hoped was listening.

"I don't know if I believe in You anymore,"

he said. "I can't see how You'd allow all of this
to happen, unless it's some kind of test.
Please, tell me this is just a test, that if we
fight hard enough, everything's going to be
okay." He drew a trembling breath, and tears
ran down his cheeks. "O Lord, after all we've
been through as a race, You can't let it end
like this. We've wandered from our purpose, I
know that. We've forgotten the one true
commandment: love. We're not so far gone,
though. This alien has helped us find love,
anew. Just two months ago, I saw Benjamin
Netanyahu sitting down to break bread with
Rami Hamdallah, grinning and laughing as if
they were longtime friends. Jesse Jackson
was an honored guest at the house of the
Grand Wizard of the KKK. We're learning to
love one another again. Please, don't let that
end here. I beg of you."

Something exploded down the street.
Well,that was that, then. Time for action.

Rev. Potts glanced up. "Thank you for
listening to me. Amen."

He stood and went to his closet. He opened
the door, unleashing the horrid stench of
stale spunk, and reached inside for Rich
Bech's parting gift to him. Slinging it on one
shoulder, he sauntered out of the rectory and
into the church where the townspeople had
crowded together for sanctuary. They all
looked up to him with tearful, scared eyes.

"It's the moment of truth, brothers and
sisters," Rev. Potts said. "Fight if you can. Or,
stay here, where it's safe. I'm going out there
and sending these sons of devils back to their

maker."

No one followed him as he walked down the center aisle, between the cluster of pews, and to the set of double doors. He eased them open and slid through, sure to close them behind him. Inside, the churchgoers rushed to the stained glass windows and tried to squint through to see what was going on.

Rev. Potts didn't have to go far. Down the block he saw one of the Xanadarians—this one disguised as Ronald Reagan—tearing a house from its very roots and throwing it at a group of people who were running away from him. It crushed them all and ended their screams immediately.

"Hey!" Rev. Potts shouted. "Those are people from *my* congregation!"

Reagan turned toward him, a stupid smile on his face. "Oh? And what are you going to do about it?"

Wow. The guy even sounded like Ronnie.

Rev. Potts shook the thought from his head and tried to think of something awesome to say. That's what happened in Hollywood, right? The good guys always had a snappy quip to say to the bad guys before killing them.

He braced Rich's bazooka on his shoulder and put his finger on the trigger. "I'm gonna' tear down this wall."

He fired.

The kickback didn't hurt as much as he'd expected, and he watched as the rocket soared at Reagan. He felt so good about his courage, he didn't even consider feeling guilty for his awful attempt at witty banter.

Reagan, annoyed, slapped at the side of the rocket, and it sailed directly into the church. The building exploded and collapsed, smoke rising from the ruin like the spirits of those who had perished within.

"No!" Rev. Potts cried. He hadn't meant for anything like this to happen. How could this guy have swatted the rocket like it had been a fly?

Bereft and broken, he could only stare at the rubble where he'd preached for decades. He didn't do anything to stop Reagan as he approached. Without a word the Xanadarian jabbed his fingers into Rev. Potts's eye sockets and pulled back hard enough to pull the Reverend's head off like it was a bowling ball. Blood jetted from the reverend's neck stump, as his body floundered around a moment before falling to the ground.

Reagan peered at the head stuck on his hand and grimaced. "Fucking pussy."

Not everyone in the church died, however. Carol Bradley, who had just seen the ruin of her mother's corpse, emerged from the wreckage and snarled at Reagan. She saw what remained of Rev. Potts, and she couldn't control herself. Her fingers hooked into claws, and she rushed the Xanadarian.

"You killed my mother, you piece of shit!" she roared.

Reagan watched with amusement as she approached, turning his folksy grin up to twenty. "Tell you what, little lady. I'll let you take the first shot.".

Carol slashed her razor-sharp fingernails at the alien, and she scored on the first go. She pierced Reagan's eye, popping it like a bubble. The Xanadarian screamed and grabbed his eye socket, feeling blood ooze against his palm.

She reared back to attack again, but Reagan saw her with his good eye. He quickly brought a foot up and kicked her between the legs hard enough that he split her in half to the throat. Shocked, she flopped to the ground, and it took her almost a minute to realize she was dead.

Reagan grimaced, as he held his hand to his eye and waited until the golden light restored it. He blinked a couple of times until the eye adjusted itself. Then he admired his handiwork. "Cunt," he said.

Just to emphasize the point he stomped her head, exploding it like a melon, before returning to his mission of complete annihilation.

In Houston, the former president knew that the Xanadarians would be coming for them. The general concurred, so they set up their defenses as best as they could. Nate asked, "Is there anything I can do?"

"Do you know how to fight?" the general asked.

"Not in the slightest."

"Then stay the fuck out of our way. Get back there with the other eggheads." He nodded to a row of consoles that most of the NASA geniuses had hidden behind.

"I'm not going to just wait to die," Nate

said. "Give me something to do."

"We need experienced soldiers up front," the general said. "You'll just get in the way. Now, go on. Get back there."

Nate wanted to argue the point, but he knew when he faced a closed mind. He'd go back for the time being, at least until he figured out something important he could do.

"You should get back there, too, Madam President," the general said.

"Nonsense. I've seen enough movies to know what I need to do. I'm a great shot with a .45, you know that. And, you don't have to call me Madam. President. I'm just—"

"You're POTUS. Anything else is a breach of protocol."

"Right. Okay then." As if she'd let this guy boss her around.

Just then the communications officer rushed over to the general. "Sir! The perimeter has been breached!"

The general shoved a cigar into his mouth and took a deep puff. Then he drew his sidearm. He knew it would do little good, but fuck it. The only alternative was to go out like a bitch, and he'd be damned if that would happen.

Another soldier looked up from a monitor. "Sir! One of them is just outside the d—"

The door cracked, and a hunk of it flew across the room, chopping the general's head off in one fell swoop. His cigar, still burning, rolled away.

Thor stood in the threshold, his hammer held in his massive, vein-covered hand. His long blond hair flowed around him in a mane pinned down by an elaborate horned helmet. He grinned, showing off teeth as big as a horse's. "Is this the best you've got? Did I just kill your finest warrior by accident? There is no sport in this."

The soldiers dropped into position and started firing at Thor. Bullets bounced harmlessly off his body as he casually strolled into the control room and brought his hammer down on the closest Marine.

Thor caught a sudden bullet in the eye, and he howled. It took him a moment to recover, but after healing himself, he started his attack with new energy, driven by anger. One by one, he turned the Marines to paste, and his hammer became redder and redder.

Nate suddenly felt inspired. He turned to the former president, recognizing a kindred spirit. He doubted the ex-leader of the free world had been in many physical fights, but he knew he'd heard one thing correctly. "Madam President, is it true that you're a dead shot with a .45? Or were you blowing smoke?"

The former president blinked, looking offended and disgusted. "Kid, I can shoot through bullet holes without hitting the edges."

"Good." He nodded toward the general's body, which still held his .45 sidearm.

"What's that going to do?" the former president asked. "You see how tough this guy is."

"His eyes are weak," Nate said.

"But he can heal himself."

"Not if we don't give him the time. Remember, Jesus said if we destroy their brains, they die."

"So?"

"So you take out both of his eyes from a distance. Then I'll run in and scramble his brains until he dies."

"With what?"

"Hey!" A voice from behind.

Nate glanced over to the whitecoats hiding behind the row of consoles. Ian poked his head out from the top.

"What?" Nate asked.

Ian threw a pen out to Nate, who caught it one handed. He glanced at it, confused. Then he almost laughed. "Okay, that's funny."

"What?" the former president asked.

"The pen is mightier than the sword. Not in this case. We need something better than this."

"Pull it apart," Ian said. "There's a knife inside. The sharpest blade I've ever encountered."

Nate yanked the two segments of the writing tool apart, and sure enough, one end held a blade in it. "Where the fuck did you get this?"

"I got mugged the last time I was in Houston," Ian said. "I didn't want it to happen again."

"So you want me to shoot Thor in the eyes so you can run over and cut his brain out?" the former president asked.

Nate offered an embarrassed shrug. "Well,

I guess."

"That's got to be the worst idea I've ever heard."

"It's better than doing nothing while this asshole kills us all."

The former president waited until Thor's attention had turned to a group of soldiers on the opposite side of the room, and then she ran to the general's corpse and grabbed the handgun.

"Hey Thor!" Nate shouted. The Xanadarian turned to face him. Nate snarled. "You suck! The Hulk's way better!"

"I don't think that's the Marvel Thor," Ian said. "I think that's the actual Norse Thor."

Nate said, "Hey Thor! I fucked Odin in his eye socket!"

Thor didn't understand any of this, but he knew it was all meant as an insult. Calmly, he gathered his hammer up and started ambling toward Nate.

The former president waited until Thor was a bit closer before she drew a bead on the god's left eye and fired. Thor screamed as he clutched at his wound, but the former president didn't give him time to recover. She sent another bullet into Thor's other eye, blinding the Xanadarian completely.

Nate rushed forward, and just before Thor could cover up the new wound, he jabbed the knife home and started stirred the Xanadarian's brain like cake batter. Blood erupted from the wound, and Thor flailed, trying to knock Nate away.

In that moment the other soldiers

understood what Nate was up to, and they rushed Thor until they swarmed hard enough to make him lose balance and fall over. They tried to hold his arms down, although his strength allowed him to fling them away rather easily. Still, he panicked, and that gave Nate enough leverage to straddle his chest and get to work stirring with Ian's knife.

Thor lashed out with his hammer, catching Nate in the chest, sending him across the room until he crashed against the wall hard enough to dent it. He bounced off and flopped to the floor with nearly all of his ribs poking out of his skin. He coughed, and blood poured from his mouth from his lacerated lungs.

The former president rushed in and kicked the knife all the way into Thor's head. Once again the Xanadarian unleashed a horrible scream, fingers scratching at his violated eye socket, trying to get the knife out. The former president squatted down and aimed the gun at the open wound.

She emptied the gun through the gaping eye socket. The onslaught was enough to turn Thor's brain to mush. He offered one final attempt to survive, flailing at the former president who easily sidestepped the attack, and then Thor's hammer fell by his side, the hand that held it lifeless.

The former president rushed to Nate's side. She knew the poor bastard's life was close to ending. No way could anyone save him at this point.

"Did we get him?" Nate spoke through a

mouth full of blood.

"We got him, son," the former president said. "You were brilliant."

"Good. Get the word out. We can beat these fuckers."

The former president gave the order, and all over the world, earth's soldiers suddenly knew how to defeat their invaders. By the time the former president looked back down at the young man with the crushed chest, Nate had expired.

She saluted the body. "That boy had more smarts than any of us combined. Let's make sure his sacrifice was not in vain. Let's kick some ass!"

"Oorah!"

Hundreds of miles away Ursula sat in the cellar of their house, clutching her boys close. Joe paced back and forth, holding his shotgun. He wanted to do more. He wanted to actively fight the invaders, but he knew his obligation was to his family. They needed his protection. Hiding down here made him feel like a coward, but he knew it was their best bet for survival.

They'd brought the TV down here with them so they could watch the news, but they'd lost power a long time ago. They tried their old radio, but the batteries were dead. Now they just waited.

The building above them started trembling. They'd dealt with a twister coming through this area before, and the house had reacted the same way. Thinking that this would be a lousy time for a tornado, Joe hugged his entire family, his back to the ceiling, so he'd take the brunt of anything that might fall on them.

The foundation cracked, and the house suddenly disappeared. Squinting through the dust cloud Joe could see that it had been flipped over on its side, revealing the cellar to the world.

Standing above them was . . . Elvis, of all people.

Joe put himself between Elvis and his family, lifting the shotgun up. "Keep back."

Elvis jumped up and hovered for a moment before floating down to the dirt floor of the cellar. Without a word, Joe put the stock to his shoulder and fired both barrels. Buckshot sprayed out, and had Elvis been an ordinary man, he would have been sporting a giant hole in the center of his body. Instead the hail bounced off of him and ricocheted back at Joe. Most of it pattered away harmlessly, but some of the balls still had enough velocity to sink into Joe's skin. He yelped, dropping the shotgun.

Taking advantage of the distraction, Elvis moved past Joe to his family. Ursula squatted down between the children, holding them close. "Why don't you leave us alone?" she asked.

"I need him." Elvis pointed to Joe. "Not you."

By now Joe recovered enough to realize what was happening. He picked up the shotgun and brandished it like a club. "Let them go. I'll leave with you if you let them be."

"You're leaving with me any way you look at it, darling." Sneering one-sided at the kids, just like the King himself.

Ethan wrestled away from Ursula's grip. Viciously, he kicked Elvis's shin. "We're gonna' kick your behind, you big jerk!"

"No!" Ursula cried. She reached out to pull her son back, but her fingers slipped off the back of his shirt.

Allen, not to be outdone by his brother, followed suit. "Yeah!" Launching his foot at Elvis.

He didn't feel their kicks. Casually, as if flicking a fly off his shoulder, he reached down and in each hand, he grabbed their respective heads. Without fanfare at all he squeezed and both their skulls popped like pimples. Brains and blood splashed all over, and oozed between Elvis's fingers.

Ursula shrieked, and Joe fell to his knees, gutted by what he'd just witnessed. No power on earth could have gotten him up on his feet in that moment. All he could see were his sons' corpses, bleeding out into the infertile dirt of the cellar.

"Shut up," Elvis said. He reared back and kicked, connecting the tip of his blue suede shoe with Ursula's chin. Her face slid up her skull and sheared away from bone. For one awful moment, she flailed with her brain flopping back and forth in the open cavity of her face, and then she fell back, twitching. Mercifully, Elvis reached in and yanked her brain out, crushing it like a beer can in his fist.

Joe whimpered, and he dared not look up into Elvis's face. All he could do was stare at those shoes, covered in blood, as more dripped down from above, pattering against the dirt like a crimson rainstorm.

"Don't worry," Elvis said. "I ain't gonna' kill you. Not yet."

"Just do it," Joe whispered.

"Excuse me?"

Joe tried to speak up, but he couldn't find his voice as it drowned in his grief.

"You'll have to say that again, partner."

Joe sobbed. "Please. I can't live without them. Just kill me."

Elvis rested a gentle hand on Joe's shoulder. "I still need you, at least for a while longer. I promise to kill you in a bit. Okay?"

Joe couldn't answer. He felt an arm wrap around his waist, and his stomach dropped as they soared up into the sky. As a kid he'd always wanted to blast through the clouds like Superman. Now? He wanted nothing more than to wink out of existence.

In New York, a couple of friends sat at the dingiest dive bar they could find, the perfect place to meet the end of the world head on. Ever since that fateful day at Joe MacDonald's farm, Eddie Taft and Haley Dean had become close friends. They wound up working together as freelancers at a lot of the same networks, and they got the feel for each others style. They drank the same slop, they hung out in the same places and, on occasion, they fucked the same prostitutes.

But, they knew the score. As soon as the attack began, they met at their favorite hangout. The bar was locked up when they arrived, but they were old hands at this sort of thing. Two crowbars and a few dips behind the bar later, and they were drinking the best rotgut this place had to offer.

"He sure got us good, didn't he?" Haley asked.

Eddie nodded. "But, it doesn't matter."

"How so?"

"Maybe he didn't intend to make the world a better place, but he did. Besides, I think he kind of likes this planet. Maybe we rubbed off on him a bit."

Haley grunted. "A lie's a lie. Don't matter who tells it."

"That's a bit closed-minded. I think his time here has changed things for the better. It sure improved my lifestyle. I didn't have to follow that asshole around all the time. He was a real piece of shit, you know?"

"This invasion crap wouldn't be happening without him. He royally fucked us. Now, we're going to die because of him. Which reminds me, we should drink faster. No telling when it'll be time for New York to go belly-up."

Eddie agreed, so he finished off his whiskey and poured another. He offered the bottle to his friend. "Maybe so, Haley. But I, for one, have enjoyed this reprieve from a world of shit. I think these past few months have been worth whatever we have coming tonight."

Haley didn't see the point in pouring

anymore, so he just started drinking from the bottle. He took a couple of swallows and smiled through the burn. "Nope. Sorry. I'm not forgiving him for this."

Eddie took a cue from his friend and reached across the bar for a fresh bottle, which he plugged into his mouth. Wiping his lips with the back of his hand, he couldn't help but smile.

"What?" Haley asked.

"You know? Just a year ago I wouldn't have had the courage to say this, but . . ."

"Say what?"

"Well, I love you."

Haley guffawed. "It's the liquor, my friend."

"No, I mean it. I love you. Before, I would have been afraid that you'd think I was, you know." He waved a hand back and forth.

Something exploded outside, and Haley turned his fearful eyes to the front windows. A dead neon Budweiser sign blocked most of the view, but they could still see fire from in here.

Then, something thumped into the side of the building hard enough to blow out the glass. Fire rushed in, and the ceiling burned in a wave, directly toward the bar.

They had no chance of getting away.

Haley turned to Eddie. "Fuck it, man. I love you, too."

They hugged each other, booze sloshing out of their bottles and onto their backs, as the fire ignited the alcohol behind the bar, completely incinerating the building in a matter of seconds.

Not too far away, Brian Murphy knelt in bed, situated between the legs of a beautiful woman he'd found in the Fox lobby earlier that evening. They'd taken a room in a nearby hotel because, for the life of him, Murphy couldn't bring himself to face his wife and kids at the end of the world. Not while knowing that they were all about to die.

Instead, he found Tracy, who once upon a time, had hit on Joe MacDonald in an attempt at getting to Jesus, and the two of them hit it off right away. At first, Murphy thought she'd want to trade for something, but who needed to barter when the apocalypse was right around the corner? They'd retired to bed and reveled in each others' flesh for as long as possible. Outside, they could hear the terrible destruction of the world. Skyscrapers came down in smoking heaps. The Statue of Liberty sank into New York Harbor. Nothing remained of Times Square except a smoking ruin and a hole halfway through the earth's crust.

But, Murphy and Tracy had each other, and they were determined to die in each others arms.

Preferably, after orgasm.

But they survived. So did the Murphy family.

Half a world away, Jamal al-Hazred rallied his soldiers against the infidel who had the nerve to pretend to be Muhammad. He led the charge with a rocket launcher, the very one he'd tried to use against Jesus months ago. It didn't work out so well for him this time, either.

Muhammad took it from him and shoved it up Jamal's ass until it came out his mouth. Jamal's men were horrified, but that didn't deter them. They fought harder. And harder. And harder. Until they too, died.

One by one, all around the world, those who had been healed by Jesus fought and died. In the space of a half an hour, the earth's population was cut down by half, and if the Xanadarians kept up the pace, the fight would be over within the hour.

In a shitsplat town in the Midwest, Antonio Santana crawled out of a bottle just in time to see the end of the world. Jesus had offered many times to cure him of his alcoholism, but he'd never wanted it. On some level, he knew he'd deserved it, especially after ruining Tammy's career when the truth came out about them.

How could he have known the guy was really Jesus? Then again, why had he needed to challenge the guy? Probably because he felt the urge to ruin lives. That's all he'd ever done as a reporter. Deep down, he enjoyed it, because he needed constant reminders that he was better than everyone else.

Except, this time it had backfired. Tammy had lost her job, and so had Antonio. Now he had nothing, and since he hadn't let Jesus heal him, no one would hire him. To put the cherry on top of this particular sundae, it looked like his violent death was at hand.

He got up the nerve to peek out through the ratty drapes of his motel room, and sure enough, the town he'd been hiding in for months was burning to the ground. Very little of it remained intact. And there! Was that . . . ? The fat guy waddling around down there, could that be Buddha?

Antonio wiped saliva from his crusty lips. Yeah, this was it. No way was he getting out of this town alive. Might as well go down swinging.

Besides, he probably had it coming.

He put on some clothes and grabbed a vodka bottle he'd finished off earlier that day. He stepped outside his motel room. At first, he panicked, wondering if he had the key on him, before he realized it didn't really matter.

When he got to the bottom of the stairs, he broke the bottle on the railing. Holding the broken remains by the handle, he advanced across the parking lot toward the Xanadarian.

Buddha, who had seen Antonio break the bottle, stopped and watched, amused. This human walked with such purpose, but booze had addled his brain so badly that he weaved back and forth like a down-and-out boxer in the last round. Finally, he stood before Buddha and held up the broken bottle like a knife.

"What are you going to do with that little French tickler?" Buddha asked.

"I'm going to feed you your ass," Antonio thought he'd said.

What he really said: "Ahmgurrahfehyeyerahhhassssssss."

Buddha laughed, ready to flick this pathetic drunk aside.

Antonio, moving with the fluid motion only an extremely angry, drunk asshole can, thrust the broken bottle over Buddha's rising hand and plunged the jagged glass into Buddha's face.

Directly into his eyes.

Buddha screamed as he put up his hands to heal himself. Antonio, using his drunken, savage wits, twisted his wrist, breaking off giant pieces of glass in Buddha's empty sockets. When Buddha clamped his hands down with the strength of a Xanadarian, he only drove the sharp spears deeper into his brain, killing himself instantly.

Antonio stared down at the corpse of Buddha, uncomprehending. Then, he looked at what remained of the broken bottle in his hand. Suddenly he understood, and he jumped up and down in victory.

"We got these sonsabitches!" he shouted. "Go for their eyes!"

He didn't notice until well after the final battle that some of the glass had worked its way into his hand. It would take months to heal properly, and by then he would be off the sauce and leading a productive life yet again.

One where he felt no need to be better than everyone else.

Jesus found Ronald McDonald on the dark side of the earth by following his vapor trail to the Eiffel Tower. In that moment, he recognized his little sister Xenthar behind the clown disguise, and he had to stop himself from laughing. The costume was ridiculous, but he knew his sister could whip the shit out of him on his best day.

He'd have to out-think her.

Xenthar squatted near the base of the Eiffel Tower and lifted with all of her strength, tearing it from its base. Then she started lifting it into the sky, where she would probably use it as a gigantic dart.

Jesus hovered at her side, smiling.

She paused, holding the Tower lazily with one hand. "Ah. Brother. Just the person I wanted to see. I promised Father that—"

Jesus deliberately broke down laughing.

"What? What's so funny?"

He forced gales of laughter out as he clutched his side with one hand and slapped his knee with the other. He kept his eyes squinted, but not so far that he couldn't see Ronald.

"Enough!" she roared. Thoughtlessly, she cast the Tower aside. It sailed across the Mediterranean, where it would eventually crash into and topple the Leaning Tower of Pisa. "Why do you laugh?"

"Your disguise," Jesus said. "Why the fuck did you pick Ronald McDonald?"

"He's one of earth's most powerful gods. He's everywhere. Not even Jesus could pull that off."

"You just don't get it. You're dressed like a clown. Do you understand?"

"You mean, a trickster."

"No. I mean a clown. He's not a god, he's a spokesman who sells cheeseburgers to kids. Weak and silly. You picked the most worthless popular culture character in this

239

planet's history."

"You . . . you lie." She didn't seem very certain, though.

"Xanadar picked Muhammad. Hell, even Father picked Elvis, and he's waaaaaay more powerful than Ronald fucking McDonald." Jesus couldn't help it anymore; he burst out into laughter again.

It had the desired effect. Ronald roared and shot herself toward him, her fist extended. Jesus ducked the blow, as he'd been expecting the attack. Then, she turned to face him again, but he was ready with a blow of his own.

He gathered all of his strength and brought both fists together in a double uppercut to the underside of her jaw. She didn't have time to defend herself. Instead, her head tore away from her shoulders with a tiny little tail of spine trailing behind. Blood gouted up from her stump as her body fell to the ground below, where it floundered around for a moment before all movement ceased.

Jesus watched as her head sailed away. He could still see the surprise on her face at the fifty-mile mark. Then, he watched the life go out of her eyes as they rolled back, showing off their pale underbellies, just before they disappeared over the horizon.

He felt a moment of sadness, then. He really hadn't wanted to do that to his sister, but she would have done the same to him. And, she might not have been so merciful. Besides, it was the way she would have wanted it. No Xanadarian wants to go out like a pussy. No, she went out in the heat of battle. Honorably.

Jesus decided to fly above the surface of the earth in search of other Xanadarians, in particular his brother. It would be best to get the battle with Muhammad out of the way. It was really the fight with his father that he feared the most. He—

"Where are you going, son?"

Jesus turned and watched as Elvis came to hover behind him. In one hand, clutched by the scruff of his neck, was Joe MacDonald. Blood covered Jesus' closest friend on earth. Closest friend *ever*.

"Put him down, Father," Jesus said. "Gently. Please. This is between you and me, not him."

"You killed your sister," Elvis said. "That wasn't very nice."

"You know I had to do it. Now please. I know you want to fight me. Let's do this."

Joe tried to speak, but they were so high up in the atmosphere that his lungs couldn't take it. Instead he thought it: *It's okay, Jesus. I don't want to live anymore.*

I will save you, Joe. I promise. Just keep silent. My father can hear us.

Elvis grinned, and Jesus could see the death behind his aviator sunglasses.

"No," Jesus said.

It's okay. Joe closed his eyes. The expression on his face seemed almost beatific, like that of a freshly martyred saint.

Elvis hooked his fingers into Joe's flesh, just above the collar bones, and yanked down as hard as he could. Every one of Joe's ribs broke as the front of his chest was torn away and sent to the ruins of Paris below. For a moment his guts remained in place, and then they unraveled and fell, blown away like streamers in the breeze.

Joe never opened his eyes again. He died before Elvis released his body.

Jesus felt empty, as if every reason to live had been taken away from him. His stomach bottomed out, and he wanted to curl up into a ball. Staring down at Joe's dwindling form as it rushed toward the ground below, Jesus couldn't believe that he'd never have a discussion with Joe MacDonald again. They'd never break bread again, they'd never go to church again and they would never again smile together.

Elvis sneered. "What are you gonna' do about it, pussy?"

Jesus hadn't been aware that he'd let his mental block down. He wasn't aware of anything else in the world. He'd barely registered that his father had spoken to him. The only thing he knew was that he felt something balled up inside his guts. It grew within him, white hot, and he could feel rage build up inside his mind, simmering almost enough to cause a distortion of the air above his head. His muscles contracted, and his bones shifted. Veins bristled underneath his skin as he bulked up, taking on more mass.

Elvis, confused, could only stare as his son transformed into a pillar of bristling muscle, bigger than any professional wrestler could ever hope for. Jesus' eyes went red, and his mouth stretched over clenched teeth. He couldn't contain himself anymore. He roared, and fire exploded from between his lips. Lasers blasted from his eyes, and Elvis's testicles shrank just a little bit.

He held up his hands, palms out in surrender. "Hold on, son—"

Jesus turned his death stare upon his father, and Elvis darted out of the way just in time to avoid getting cut in two by the rays and flames. He didn't evade Jesus himself, though, as his son hurtled through the sky with both fists thrust out in front of himself, plowing Elvis in the stomach with a double punch.

Elvis flew across the hemisphere, barely comprehending what had just happened. Jesus followed, driven by high octane rage and an unfathomable pain.

All around the world, the last of the Xanadarians stopped battling the earthlings. They tuned in to the two-fisted battle between father and son. They watched in horror as the strongest of their kind—their very king—was punched so hard he got stuck in earth's orbit and circled the planet in three seconds flat.

They'd all heard the rumors, but Jesus had been so always been so pathetic that they assumed it couldn't be true. Their dead sibling—the second born—had to have not been counted in the birth order. Jesus couldn't really be the seventh son of a seventh son.

Yet here he was, swollen like a gladiator, kicking seven shades of shit out of his own father. Every time Elvis came to a stop, Jesus was there to pound him again. With each punch, he hit his father so hard he created a new universe, whose inhabitants would never understand how it came to be.

Addled, Elvis managed to find his feet, and he neatly sidestepped his son's next attack. Not that it mattered. Jesus simply turned his head, and the death rays in his eyes did all the work. This time they sliced through Elvis's left hand, and pieces of his fingers rained down to the ocean below.

Elvis howled, but he didn't give Jesus the satisfaction of giving an inch. Instead, he regrouped and landed a roundhouse kick to Jesus' nuts.

It had no effect.

Jesus brought both fists down like a hammer onto Elvis's head, and the sound wave from the blow exploded every glass object in the solar system. Elvis, senseless, dropped from the sky. Just before he hit the surface of the ocean, he pulled himself out of a nose dive and flew for the nearest cover: New York City.

Jesus turned his head, and his death rays sliced Elvis's feet off at the shins. Again, Elvis screamed, but he did not alter his course. In seven seconds he came down in Midtown Manhattan so hard he plowed up the entirety of Fifth Avenue just as easily as if it had been fertile ground.

Three seconds later Jesus came down, and

he turned his eyes on the Empire State Building, slicing through it at the foundation. Then, before it could topple, he closed his eyes and stuck his fingers in the cut he'd made, lifting the entire skyscraper out of the ground.

Elvis glanced up in horror as Jesus brought the entire building down on him like a gigantic club, destroying everything in sight.

Not that there was much of New York left to destroy.

At the very center of it all, Elvis stared up at the sky, crippled but still alive. He whimpered, turning his head around, trying to get the rest of his body to crawl away. That was all he *could* move.

Jesus, huffing and out of breath, stood over his father. His death rays cut into Elvis's chest, destroying the heart in a split second. But, he knew even that wouldn't finish the old bastard off.

He fell to his knees, careful to keep his death rays aimed low, and without looking, he grabbed both sides of his father's head and plunged his thumbs into Elvis's eyes through the aviator glasses. Both the lenses and the eyes exploded, and Jesus screamed fire and death into his father's face as he pulled his hands apart. Elvis's skull split down the middle, and his brain tumbled out onto the rotten street, where it sizzled and popped inside a stream of Jesus' fiery breath.

Elvis shifted and sputtered, and the illusion fell away. Xanadar lay before the universe, dead and naked. King no more.

Jesus didn't have time to celebrate. Before he had a second to congratulate himself, something powerful exploded against the back of his neck. He stumbled forward, and his death rays blinked out. The fire stopped coming from his mouth. His body deflated, returning to its original size.

Muhammad stood over him, seething. His fists opened and closed as he dropped the M1 Abrams tank he'd used to knock his brother down. "You killed our father."

Groaning, Jesus sat up, looking at his brother. "Yeah. He killed my best friend."

"He killed a fucking earthling. Who gives a shit about them? You killed your own kind! The highest crime you could commit!"

A lopsided grin formed on Jesus' face. "That's no way to talk to your king, brother."

"King?!" Muhammad's eyes went wide, and if he could have killed Jesus with a glare, he would have. "I'm the oldest. He named me his inheritor."

"Now *you're* thinking like a human. I killed him. That means I replace him. Or have you forgotten?" Jesus blew him a kiss.

Now it was Muhammad's turn to smile. No humor danced in his eyes, though. "Xanadar was old. Almost feeble. His time was up. Now you face Xanadar—his first born—and I am at the prime of my game."

Oh shit. Jesus handled Elvis just fine, but that was because he'd been granted superpowers by his grief. Now he was just his regular old self, and he knew his brother could take him any day of the week. He concentrated on generating his eye lasers, but nothing happened. He thought of Joe's death again, but he was no longer able to bulk up.

Muhammad grabbed Jesus by the shirt and yanked him to his feet. "Any last words, brother?"

Jesus remembered Rich's last gesture toward Muhammad, and he drew in breath to spit in his brother's face. Muhammad saw it coming, though, and he reared back, ducking the wad of saliva. He lurched forward, throwing an uppercut into Jesus' jaw, sending him skyward, almost into orbit. Jesus had the chance to fill his lungs just before Muhammad launched himself against him, blasting the both of them into space.

You scared yet, brother? Muhammad asked.

Fffffuck youuuuuu.

Muhammad hit him again, and Jesus felt himself sail across the stars. He felt the moon's gravity latch onto him and pull him down gently toward the surface. Then, Muhammad kicked him so hard Jesus crashed into the moon, creating a new crater that went almost all the way down to the core. He barely managed to keep breathing, as he tried to pull himself out of the hole.

Muhammad grabbed him by the neck and yanked him out. *You're the king of jack shit.*

Fuck this banter. Jesus jabbed Muhammad in the eye as hard as he could, popping it and driving it back into his skull. Muhammad gritted his teeth, but he didn't scream. Instead he yanked Jesus' finger out and bit it off at the root.

Jesus moaned, and lost some air. He held onto most of it despite the incredible pain in his hand.

Muhammad chewed his brother's flesh and theatrically swallowed it. *That the best you got, little brother?*

Blood bubbled out of Jesus' wound and floated away. Again, Jesus chose to respond with action instead of words; he stuck his bloody hand in Muhammad's face, momentarily blinding him. Muhammad lashed out, but Jesus was too quick. He escaped his brother's grip and grounded himself, hoping for more leverage.

Then, just as Muhammad cleared the blood from his remaining eye, Jesus crouched down and threw the hardest double uppercut he could. It caught Muhammad on the chin, and he sailed away from the moon. He struggled to gain control of his momentum, but speeding quickly out of the moon's gravitational pull, he could do nothing but enjoy the ride.

Jesus aimed himself carefully, and when he'd aligned with his brother, he crouched down and pushed off from the moon with all his might. He sailed past the earth and caught up with his brother around Venus. He drove his body into Muhammad, and Muhammad— with his newfound momentum—was driven directly through Mercury, leaving the planet looking like a doughnut.

Jesus rested on the surface of the ruined planet, looking out at his flailing brother floating helplessly in space. This close to the sun, everything practically boiled uncontrollably, and Jesus—as strong and as nigh-invincible as he was—wanted to melt.

Any last words, brother? Jesus asked.

You can't kill me! You're not strong enough, not when you're like this!

Out here I don't need strength. Jesus jumped away from Mercury, darting toward his brother. When he got close enough he turned himself around and drove his foot into Muhammad's stomach. Using the momentum from this strike, Jesus floated back toward Mercury as he watched his brother, bent over, sail backwards.

Muhammad looked at Jesus with his good eye. Jesus looked back, smiling.

Fuck you, Muhammad said.

Then, he fell into the sun, where he disintegrated within a millisecond.

Exhausted, Jesus let himself fall to Mercury, where he rested. Tears welled up in his eyes as he realized what he'd just done. Not only had he lost his closest friend, he'd also laid waste to his family. Things would never be the same.

His breath threatened to run out soon, so he leaped away from Mercury and aimed himself at earth. In about ten minutes he found himself caught up in its gravitational pull, and when he could breathe again, he let out the stale air in his lungs,sobbing. Tears poured out of him as he floated back to the earth's surface.

He landed in the ruins of the MacDonald

farm, and cried his eyes out. He collapsed into a pile, and let the grief and sorrow pour out of him, dripping into the fertile ground beneath him, where next year a fresh crop would grow, the strongest the earth had ever known.

Then he became aware that the surviving Xanadarians had surrounded him. He could see the fear etched in their faces. Not only had he completely obliterated his brother, generally considered the most dangerous of his kind, he'd also killed his father, the strongest. None of them could do a goddam thing to him, and they knew it.

"Go," he whispered.

None of them moved.

Then, as if possessed by his new station in life, he rose like a beast. "I am your king! You will do as I say!"

They all backed away. One of them said, "Where?"

Jesus spat. "Home. Go home. You'll receive further instructions later."

"But earth—"

"Earth is not ours. Now go."

They looked at each other uncertainly, but one look into Jesus' set face, and they knew there would be no more discussion. One by one, they drew breath and took off for space. He watched them go, and felt nothing but disgust for his own kind.

And sorrow for his adoptive people.

For Joe MacDonald.

And Jesus wept.

CHAPTER 18:
THE FINAL GIFT

One week later, Jesus sat in the bathtub of his room at the Diaghilev, soaking. Even now, his muscles ached, but he didn't give them much thought. All he could think about was Joe MacDonald, about how he'd gone back to Paris to pick up his only friend's remains. How he'd cradled the mess who had been the first man to greet him on this planet.

Just moments before, he'd gone to the MacDonald home to break the bad news, and he saw what his father had done to Joe's wife. To his kids. Any last piece of a soul he had left by that point slipped away from him like smoke through the skeletal branches of a dead tree.

He wished he'd never come to this planet. Falling in love with these people hurt too much, especially now that most of them were dead and gone. To have never loved them would have been better. That way, it wouldn't have fucked with him so badly when his fellow Xanadarians would have eventually laid waste to earth.

He'd never felt so miserable in two thousand years. By the standards of the earthlings, he had superpowers. The only superpower he wanted now was the ability to turn back time and do it all over again.

He knew his motives were selfish, and he didn't care. He only wished he could have skipped the whole thing.

Two days ago, he'd laid the remains of his surrogate family to rest on their farm. The former president had a monument to them built over their grave, where it would stand for the rest of human memory. Now, he prepared himself for another Sermon on the Mount.

Weakly, he pulled the plug on the drain and stood, reaching for a towel. As he dried himself off, he looked into the mirror and saw deep pouches under his eyes. His body looked hollow, as if he was barely there. Fixing the illusion wouldn't have been a problem, but he didn't care. He looked like he thought he *should* look.

He dressed in his robes and gave his reflection one last glance. Yes, everything looked perfect. Symbolic.

The former president waited outside the door to the hotel room. When she saw Jesus emerge, she snapped to attention. "You ready?"

Jesus couldn't speak. He only nodded his head.

They walked to the elevator, which they took down to the lobby. Outside, a car awaited them, and it took them back out to the Mount of the Beatitudes. Police had blocked off the roads, so they could get there without getting stuck in traffic. A good thing, too, since so many turned out for this one. Thousands of humans gathered around the tiny hill, where Jesus had stopped people from building a monument to himself. He couldn't stand anything like that. It sounded like the kind of thing his father would have done.

Even worse, it fed the delusion that he really *was* Jesus Christ. Despite the televised confession, most of the world still thought of him as their Lord and savior.

The driver pulled over behind the hill, and the former president escorted Jesus to the top. Once he arrived, the crowd roared their adulation so loudly that Jesus could feel their voices thrumming through his emaciated chest. It made his heart pump harder, until he felt a rush. It felt like being possessed.

He fought back the sensation.

The former president waved to everyone before retreating, leaving Jesus on the stage alone. A sound system had been put up, since not even Jesus could project his voice across tens of thousands of people and get everyone to hear him.

He stepped up to the microphone. "Hello, everyone."

"HELLO!" everyone cried out in at least a dozen different languages.

"A lot has happened since the last time I talked to you all from this mount. A lot of it has been terrible. We've all lost loved ones in

253

the war for earth's independence, and I'm terribly sorry for bringing my brothers here."

An odd feeling came over him. As he looked across the crowd he realized that just a year ago, these people were all rabid enemies. Now they'd united as one, and their love radiated from them.

Maybe all of this wasn't for nothing.

"I'm kind of glad I came here, though," he said. He surprised himself by actually believing this. "If I hadn't, they would have come here first, and they would not have been very nice. They would have crushed you. Enslaved you. Killed you, in the end. This planet would be the third cinder from the sun, not the lush place it is now. Instead, though the trials and tribulations have been difficult, this planet has risen from the muck of its own hatred. I look out at you all and see your love, brighter than a thousand suns, and I'm humbled."

The crowd cheered, and the wave of their love nearly crippled Jesus. He struggled not to tear up.

When he felt like he could comfortably continue speaking: "I have to leave you now. I feel like there isn't anything more I can do here. The road to healing and reconstruction is long, but now that you have love in your hearts again I think you'll get the job done."

He gave them a moment to process this before continuing: "My home planet is in a lot more trouble than earth is. As you know I'm now the king of my people. Word has gotten back to me that they've already renamed my world Xathus for me. We have a long history of power struggles, violence, greed and insanity, and it's now my job to untangle the mess. I have to change things for them, or they'll be twisted by their own misguided desires. I couldn't do that before, but now that I'm king I'm in a position where I can rewire my society. I have to take that chance."

They cried out "no" and "don't leave us" and "we love you," but Jesus had to harden his heart against them. He held up a hand. "This is something I must do. My people's history is even longer than yours, but the work I've done here has convinced me that I can make a difference."

"Jesus! Stay with us!"

Jesus drew in a breath and let it out. "I am not Jesus Christ, as I have told you before. Are there any gods? Much less One True God? I don't know. I've been around a long time. So have my people. We have no gods in our culture. If they exist, we've never met them. I recommend that you live your lives as if they don't exist. Don't be good because you're afraid of being punished. Do good because you *are* good. Don't commit terrible acts and then confess them for the sake of unburdening your soul. Confess to those you have wronged. The misdeeds of people can only be worked out amongst themselves."

Everyone cheered.

"I hope Jesus existed," Jesus continued. "He seemed like a decent guy. He's credited with saying one of the most beautiful things a human being has ever said. So I close with this final word, a direct quote: 'A new commandment I give unto you, that ye love one another.'"

The crowd roared with such approval that the soundwave nearly blew Jesus back a step. Feelings of love crowded him so much that he felt claustrophobic. He couldn't take it anymore. He'd meant to say goodbye, with maybe a vague promise of returning someday, but he couldn't. Not now.

Instead he crouched down and shot himself up into the sky. The earthlings screamed after him. A child shouted, "Jesus! Come back!"

He couldn't face them. He had to get away. Before leaving, he'd intended to make one final stop by the MacDonalds' grave, but he'd been too overwhelmed. It would be best to just leave.

Jesus shed his disguise and took a deep breath before he broke free from Earth's atmosphere. He jetted out into deep space, faster than he'd ever moved, and though he wanted to look back for one last glimpse, he didn't.

He couldn't.

EPILOGUE

Four generations later, after all those who remembered actually seeing Jesus Christ had passed away, earth and its occupants went back to their old destructive ways and set themselves back on the path to corruption.

"So it goes."
-Kurt Vonnegut, *Slaughterhouse-Five*

THE END

About the Author

John Bruni is the author of *Tales of Questionable Taste*, a collection of horror and bizarro stories from StrangeHouse Books, and *Strip*, an ultra-violent and hyper-sexed crime novel from Musa. His work has appeared in a number of publications, most notably *Shroud*, *Hardboiled*, *Cthulhu Sex* and others, including anthologies such as *Vile Things* from Comet Press, *A Hacked-Up Holiday Massacre* from Pill Hill and *Strange Fucking Stories* from StrangeHouse. He lives in Elmhurst, IL, and he's very proud of himself for doing the research to make this monster smut as true to Mary Shelley's novel as possible.